It was as a teacher tha
the two girls whose tru_ story inspired
the novel *Instant Sisters*. But Rose had
plenty of her own material to draw on,
having shared not just a bedroom, but a
bed with her own sister for twelve years.
They didn't always get on and bedtime
was sometimes a battlefield, with Rose
drawing the line down the bed, which
her sister's cold feet always crossed.

Rose has two adult daughters – who, as
children, didn't have to share a bed.
She lives in Leicester where, despite the
fact she's written more stories about
animals than anyone she knows, she
lives alone, with no pets!

to Rachel and Charlotte –
two real sisters.

ORCHARD BOOKS
96 Leonard Street, London EC2A 4XD
Orchard Books Australia
32/45-51 Huntley Street, Alexandria, NSW 2015
ISBN 1 84362 199 1
First published in Great Britain in 1989
This edition published in 2003
Text © Rose Impey 1989
Cover illustration © Goldy Broad 2003
The right of Rose Impey to be identified as the author of this work
has been asserted by her in accordance with the
Copyright, Designs and Patents Act, 1988.
A CIP catalogue record for this book is available from the British Library.
1 3 5 7 9 10 8 6 4 2
Printed in Great Britain

Instant
SISTERS

rose impey

ORCHARD BOOKS

o n e

Tina lay in the bottom bunk, hiding under her quilt. Above her Joanne was reading and had been for most of an hour.

'Can we have the light off soon?'

'I'm reading.'

'I know that, but I want to get to sleep.'

'Is somebody stopping you?'

'The light's stopping me.'

The light snapped off, Joanne's book hit the floor, and she threw herself violently back onto her pillow, causing the bunk beds to sway from side to side.

'Satisfied?'

Tina didn't answer. She didn't really expect sleep to come easily, but she needed to be in the dark, so that she could think about what had happened. She could concentrate better in the dark; there were fewer distractions.

Joanne lay tense and angry. She would have preferred the distractions; she didn't want to think things through. She wanted to pretend they had never happened. She would have kept on reading until sleep defeated her and the book actually fell from her hand, if she'd been allowed to choose.

The two girls lay there wide awake, determined not to speak. But they could hear one another quite clearly: breathing, turning in bed, coughing. Every sound seemed amplified.

Tina closed her eyes and tried to pretend she was at home in her own bed. The thought brought a swell of sadness which almost made her gasp. She turned over and started to suck her thumb.

Joanne's voice cut through the darkness. 'You're never going to do that every night, are you?'

Tina's heart leapt. 'Do what?'

'Make that foul row.'

Tina didn't reply, but she took her thumb out and dried it on her pyjamas.

'You're twelve, nearly thirteen for goodness sake; only babies suck their thumbs.'

'I can't get to sleep if I don't.'

'Well, tough luck. If you think I'm going to lie here listening to you slopping and slurping, you've got another think coming.'

It felt as though Joanne had slapped her. 'I didn't ask to come here, you know. I don't like having to share any better than you do,' said Tina.

Joanne sat straight up in bed. 'Oh, you can't begin to imagine how much I hate it.' She lay back and closed her eyes. This must be what it's like to be in prison, she thought, stuck with some stranger you can't bear the sight of. But at least in prison you aren't expected to be friends. Nobody expects you to enjoy it!

Joanne's mum had talked about it as if it was going to be a kind of treat. 'It'll be good for you, Joanne. Tina'll be company, like having a sister.'

Sister! Joanne shuddered. She turned over noisily, fluffed up her pillows, and dragged her quilt about the bed, before finally settling down.

Below her, Tina lay still wide awake, going over the events of the day. It had seemed like any other Saturday in the summer holidays, stretching before her, long and uneventful. But it had surprised her; it had proved to be the most eventful day of her life.

She'd got up late, partly for lack of anything else to do, but partly because of the terrible row between her mum and dad the night before. She wanted to keep out of the way until it all blew over. But this time it hadn't blown over.

Tina had lost count of the number of times her dad had threatened to leave; now he really meant it. And he was taking her with him.

He came into her room. 'Have you finished, love? Because if you have we might as well go. I've rung Helen; she's expecting us.'

'I don't know what to take. I can't get it all in.'

'Just take what you need for the weekend. I can come back and get things later.'

The case wouldn't close. Her dad put his full weight onto it, fastened the catches and picked it up.

'What the heck have you got in here?'

'Nothing much: some clothes, CDs, Sammy's food and bedding.'

'You can't take that hamster, no way.'

'I can't go then,' she said, and burst into tears.

'Come on.' Her dad put his arm round her.

'I don't want to go, Dad.'

'I know you don't, but I've done things I didn't want to do for years, for your sake, and Sharon's. I've tried to get along with your mam, you know I have.' Tina nodded. 'Well then, love, now it's my chance. Don't you think you owe it me?' Tina sighed. ''Cause if you won't come with me, I can't go. I can't leave you here. Promise me you'll just give it a try.'

Tina nodded. She didn't know what else she could do.

An hour later they arrived at Helen's front door, carrying two cases and a hamster cage. It felt to Tina as if they were going on holiday. Helen opened the door, Joanne appeared behind her mum.

'Well, we're here. I'm sorry about the animal, love. D'you still want us?'

'Oh, Dave, of course I do. Come on in.' They kissed each other, there on the doorstep for anyone to see. Tina and Joanne looked away, too embarrassed to watch. Then they all went in.

It was a terraced house, dark inside at first, but when they got through to the living room at the back it was much brighter. It seemed to Tina very tidy and rather posh.

'Sit down. I'll make you a drink,' said Helen. 'You can put that down, you know.'

But Tina perched on the edge of her chair, clutching the hamster's cage as if she feared someone might steal it.

She was noticing all the details which made this house so different from her own: the way the wallpaper and the curtains were the same colour as the carpet, and the shelves on the walls were full of books. Instead of the kind of clutter she was used to on top of cupboards – pairs of tights, make-up, washing waiting to be ironed – there were just a few ornaments and a couple of photographs in frames. And when the tea came, the biscuits were on a plate, not handed round in the packet like at home.

'I've started sorting the beds,' said Helen. 'You girls won't have to mind sharing; we've only got the two rooms.' She deliberately didn't look at Joanne; she already knew her opinion.

'Course they won't,' said Dave, answering for them. 'They'll love it, two girls, same age. Give them a couple of hours together and they'll be up to all sorts of tricks.' The girls looked horrified at this suggestion, but neither of them spoke.

'Well, we'll just finish off then. Come on, Joanne.'

When they'd gone upstairs, Dave said, 'Don't look so fed up, sweetheart. You'll soon get used to each other.'

'No we won't.'

'Come on, Tina. I couldn't have left you at home. Your mam's not up to looking after herself, never mind you. You're better off here with me.'

Tina wanted to contradict her dad, but she knew he was right; her mum had got much worse lately. She hardly even seemed to take in the fact that they were leaving. She just kept on looking out of the window as if she was expecting someone. She was there physically, but the real person inside her seemed to have disappeared, leaving some stranger instead, like a caretaker.

Tina was glad that Sharon was staying there, to keep an eye on their mum. Sharon was nearly sixteen and old enough to choose for herself. But there had been no choice for Tina. She was here, whether she liked it or not.

*

Later in the evening Helen led them upstairs. Dave carried the cases; Tina carried Sammy. The four of them crowded into the small back bedroom, looking at the arrangements Helen had made.

'It's going to be a bit of a tight squeeze, I'm afraid, even without that hamster.'

'No, love, it's cosy,' said Dave. He put his arm round Helen.

'I'll keep him under the bed,' said Tina

'You will not,' said Joanne.

'Now be reasonable . . .' said Helen.

'She can put it in that corner, under those drawers. I don't want it anywhere near me.'

Helen sighed.

'Don't worry, they'll soon be the best of friends. It's not as if they don't know each other,' Dave assured her.

'We don't *know* each other,' said Joanne.

'You know what I mean. You're not strangers.'

But Joanne felt that they might just as well have been. They had spent the last year in the same class at the comprehensive school, but they'd hardly ever spoken. They'd had no reason to. They had been neither friends nor enemies – until now.

'Well, we'll leave you to get yourselves sorted out,' said Helen.

'Get to know each other better,' said Dave, making

both girls cringe. As the door closed behind him, the girls caught each other's eye and abruptly looked away.

They stood around in the bedroom; there didn't seem to be anything to sort out.

'You've got your own computer,' Tina said.

'Yes. And it cost a lot of money so I'd rather you didn't touch it.'

'What would I want to do that for?' Tina was not impressed by computers. 'Haven't you got a CD player?'

'No.'

'Where do you play your CDs?'

'I don't like pop music.'

Tina couldn't tell if this was a joke or not, but guessed it wasn't.

'What *do* you like doing, then?'

'Minding my own business mainly.'

This effectively put an end to the conversation. Both girls looked away. The silence went on for several minutes.

'You can have that drawer to put your things in.' Joanne indicated a drawer in the bottom of the wardrobe.

But Tina said, 'No thanks.' She didn't intend staying here; she saw no point in unpacking. She pushed her case under the bed.

As soon as she thought it was reasonable, she told Joanne she was tired. She undressed in the bathroom, rather than let Joanne see her in her underwear, then hurried into bed and turned her face to the wall. It had seemed a long day and she was glad it was nearly over.

She lay in the strange bedroom, which was dark now and quiet. Even the darkness was denser than at home; the curtains were thicker. And the outside noises she could hear were different: there were no children playing in the street, no droning of speed boats on the nearby gravel pits, no comforting sound of television downstairs.

Tina felt under the bed to check her case was still there. She ran her hand over the catches. She wouldn't unpack it. She would be ready for the moment when Dave said she could go home.

At last sleep began to overtake her. She made little sighing noises as she drifted off, automatically putting in her thumb.

'Oh God,' Joanne groaned. 'How pathetic.'

She wondered how long she was going to have to share her room with this...wimp. She was beginning to realise how much she needed her privacy.

As an only child Joanne had often dreamed about having a sister to play with and tell secrets to. When she was younger she'd invented one. She'd set a place at the table for this imaginary child, put clothes out for her to wear each morning, even shared her sweets into equal piles. But now she was older, Joanne had got used to being alone. And she preferred it that way.

It was typical of adults, she thought, not to realise. They thought they could stick the two of them together and expect them instantly to like each other. Well, it wouldn't work. It was like all that 'instant' stuff – a complete sham.

Joanne pictured those instant cake mixes that promised success in minutes. And what did you really end up with? A kind of stodgy mess that tasted like foam rubber. Joanne had once had an argument with Helen over them, in a supermarket. She'd tried to persuade her mum to buy one.

'They're rubbish,' Helen insisted. 'A waste of money. I can help you make a proper cake.'

But that's exactly what Joanne didn't want. She didn't want Helen watching her, explaining every step in that patient teacherish voice of hers. She wanted to do it all by herself. So Helen had relented.

When they got home Joanne went straight into the kitchen, telling Helen to keep out. And it was made in minutes. Then she'd bravely tried to eat it but the cake died in her mouth and she had to keep drinking mouthfuls of water to help her swallow it.

'Anything worthwhile takes a bit of time and effort,' Helen told her, yet again. 'There isn't much instant success in life, Joanne.' And she'd known her mum was right.

So why hadn't Helen seen that now, instead of throwing them in together like this?

It was an Instant Recipe for Disaster.

Ingredients: Two girls with not one thing in common.

Method: Mix them together, forcing them into the smallest space you can find. Then simply leave them alone, to suffer in silence, preferably overnight for best results.

And what would they end up with? Not sisters, that was for sure, not even friends.

Probably Instant Enemies.

t w o

Tina raced home from school as she always did on a Friday. She took her mum's front door key out of her purse and let herself in. The minute she closed the door she began to smile. This first hour, when she had the house to herself, was the best part of her week. Seeing her mum's weekly accumulation of clutter always comforted her.

Even after eight months of living apart, this evidence of her mum's life going on as usual without her could give Tina a little ache, but at the same time it made her feel reassured to know that her mum was still here, if she ever needed her.

It was an understanding between them that her mum could leave the tidying up until she came to visit each Friday. Tina looked forward to doing it. This had been the pattern ever since she and Dave had gone to live at Helen's, and Tina had fallen into it quite easily.

First she collected the coffee cups and plates scattered around the house, emptied ashtrays and cleared surfaces. She hid things in cupboards, trying to create the same kind of order that she was now used to at Helen's. She washed the pots and put them away. Then she made her mum's bed and hung up the clothes which lay in heaps on the bedroom floor. She never went into Sharon's room, that was something else that was understood between them.

While she worked, Tina put some music on really loud. Sometimes she sang or danced, holding up her mum's clothes in front of her as a partner. She talked to herself, keeping up a one-sided imaginary conversation with her mum.

'*I* don't know. This is a fine mess. If it wasn't for me nothing would get done in this house. What did your last servant die of? Overwork?'

Tina stopped to listen to herself and realised how much she sounded like Helen. It wasn't only the words, but the tone of her voice too. She looked around embarrassed, half expecting to see someone peering in through the window.

It was just part of the game she liked to play: pretending that she was the grown-up and her mum was the one who needed looking after. Her mum didn't seem to mind playing that game, even now that she was so much better, but everyone else still treated Tina as if she was a baby and that irritated her.

In the last year she felt she had grown up a lot. Since she had gone to live at Helen's so many things had changed. *She* had certainly changed, inside if not out. It was this *inside* Tina that she felt closest to now. It was almost a different personality she could take out sometimes and try on, like a set of someone else's clothes. If Joanne had crept up and looked through the window on a Friday afternoon, she would never have recognised Tina.

At five o'clock Tina put on the kettle, so that she could have a cup of tea ready for her mum. Having finished the smaller chores, she began to notice the bigger cleaning jobs which desperately needed doing, the windows, the cooker, the carpets, but her mum wouldn't let her do any of these.

'No point bothering. I shan't be here much longer. Anyway that hoover's very temperamental. When I get a flat I'll have all the equipment: I shall have a dishwasher, a washing machine and a tumble-drier, Kev says – if I want one.'

Kev was her mum's boyfriend. Tina wasn't sure what she thought about Kev. Sometimes he was good fun; he had pretend fights with her. He aimed fake blows all over body until she didn't know where to defend herself next, then he darted in past her guard, and tickled her until she begged him to stop. And even then sometimes he wouldn't.

He had wanted to be a boxer, but instead he drove enormous trucks. He owned a car and a motorbike and once, when he'd given Tina a ride on it, he'd leaned so low around corners that the footrest had scraped on the road, making sparks. She'd been nearly sick with fear.

Her mum had only laughed at her. 'What a carry on. You were perfectly safe. Kev knows what he's doing.' But Tina had never ridden behind him again. She had a feeling she couldn't really explain, that there was something scary about Kev, almost dangerous.

Very occasionally, if something upset him, he got angry. Not in the way Dave did, fizzing up like a bottle of pop, but quietly and slowly, smouldering on a long fuse. He was like those fireworks which you keep expecting to go off, but don't, leaving you feeling nervous and edgy. On these occasions Tina kept well clear of him.

Tina wasn't really looking forward to living with Kev, but if she wanted to come home to her mum she had no choice.

'When me and Kev get married and get a decent flat, then you can come back,' her mum had recently promised her. 'It won't be long now. But don't say anything to Kev; I haven't told him yet. And don't tell your dad neither. It's our secret.'

Of course Tina hadn't told Kev, or her dad; she hadn't told anyone, even though sometimes she felt so full of the secret she could almost burst.

Tina heard the door open. Her mum walked in,

dropping bags of shopping on the kitchen floor.

'I sometimes think I should have been born a donkey, all the carrying I do.' Tina gave her mum a hug and a kiss. She gently eased Tina off. She found this cuddling a bit awkward, now that Tina was nearly as big as she was. 'Where's that cuppa? I'm parched.'

Tina poured a cup of tea. While her mum drank it, she unpacked the shopping and put it away.

'What kind of a week have you had?' Tina asked.

Her mum's account was full of minor aches and pains and a long story about someone she worked with who was having an affair with the manager and so was getting preferential treatment in the shop. When at last she had exhausted the story she asked, 'What about you?'

'All right,' Tina shrugged, 'except for Joanne. I'm sick of her, always getting at me, calling me stupid.'

'Like her mother, thinks she's cleverer than anybody else, thinks she's a flaming expert on everything.'

Tina sighed. Her mum was off already. She never seemed to listen really attentively, unless Tina began to complain about Helen, even indirectly like this. She was getting quite clever at turning the conversation round to Helen, regardless of where it had started.

Tina tried to distract her, before she got too involved. 'What are we having for tea, Mum?'

'Now what do you think we're having?' her mum teased her

It was an unnecessary question because every Friday they had the same. It was a ritual; tinned hotdogs with lots of onions and tomato sauce in soft white rolls, followed by a bar of chocolate, eaten on their knees in front of the television. Tina loved it. It was the kind of food Helen wouldn't let them have. She hated anything she considered to be junk food and refused to buy it.

Once, when Tina told her mum this, she said, 'I don't know what she's talking about – junk food! I got these sausages in Tesco's; this bread's fresh today.'

So Tina had repeated what Helen thought about white bread having no real food value, and what she always said if she or Joanne ever asked for sausages. Helen had watched a documentary on television which told you in graphic detail what they really put into some sausage meat, and she'd never bought a sausage since.

Tina listed it for her mum: 'As well as the meat they use gristle, powdered bone and hair, the stomach and all the innards – everything. They grind it all down in a huge machine. They don't leave anything out, even the blood.'

'Oh, do stop it,' said her mum, 'you're making me feel sick.' But, even so, she'd put the sausages in one frying pan and fried the onions in another, with pork dripping, until they were soft and shiny. Then she and Tina had settled down with a glass of Coke each and watched TV.

'Junk food indeed!' her mum grumbled on. 'Judging by the look of her, she could do with a bit of junk food inside her. She's like one of them starving Africans, all bone and no bust.'

Tina soon regretted ever having mentioned the subject. Now her mum often referred to it. But today her mum didn't seem interested in anything. Her hotdog lay hardly touched on the plate. She looked pale and tired.

'Do you want it, love? I'm not feeling very hungry. I've been a bit off it all week. I think it must be a bug or something.'

Tina took it. She was always hungry on a Friday. She felt guilty, enjoying the hotdog so much, knowing what Helen would think if she saw her.

'You put your feet up,' she told her mum, 'and I'll make you a cuppa and do the washing up.'

'No, I'm going to have a bath, before Sharon gets in and uses up the water.'

'You're not going out, are you?'

'Kev's coming, we're going down the club, so you'll have to go a bit earlier tonight. You don't mind, just this once, do you, love?'

Tina didn't show her mum that she minded, but she did. It wasn't just this once, it happened quite often on a Friday. She had so little time with her that she begrudged losing any of it. It felt comfortable and relaxing being here and Tina wished she didn't have to go back at all. This was where she belonged.

Now that her mum was in the bath, she suddenly remembered she hadn't asked if there was any news about the flat. Surely, if there had been, she'd have said.

Tina heard Sharon let herself in. She got up and went through to put the kettle on, to brew up again. She wondered who did these jobs when she wasn't here.

'Hi, little 'un,' said Sharon. She gave Tina a hug and then dropped onto the settee. 'I'm absolutely done in. Where's our mam?'

'In the bath,' said Tina. She gave Sharon a cup of tea. 'Kev's coming. They're going out.'

'So, what's new? They go out most nights. That's no reason for her to hog the hot water.' Tina kept quiet. She tried never to get drawn into arguments between her mum and Sharon. 'Anyway, how are you?'

'All right,' Tina shrugged. 'Dad sent his love.' Sharon turned away angrily; she studied a point on the wall above the clock. 'Can't you just say hello, this once?'

'What on earth for?' Sharon snapped.

'Then he'll know you don't blame him.'

'But I do blame him. And there's no need to look at me like that. I can't understand why you should worry about it; I don't. A few more months and I won't have to be involved at all.'

This was what Sharon was really waiting for – total independence. She had lots of plans for her future: they involved making plenty of money and eventually travelling as far away from here as she could. She behaved as if she had never heard of the unemployed. Even though she was still in her last year at school she already had a number of jobs: every night she worked from four till six at a local petrol station, on Saturdays she worked in a shoe shop in town, on Sunday mornings she served, unofficially, in the off-licence down the road, and most nights of the week she was out babysitting with her boyfriend Pete. Sharon was sixteen and already in charge of her own life.

Tina knew she really ought to drop the subject, but she said, 'I don't understand why you blame Dad. It wasn't all his fault. I feel sorry for him as well...'

'You know your trouble, don't you, you work too hard at seeing everybody else's point of view. It's not a good idea. It's hard enough for kids like us. Look how you've been messed about and uprooted. Don't make it any harder for yourself...'

'Yes, but I can't help...'

'It's black and white, Tina. *He* walked out on *her*. He left her, even though he knew she wasn't in any state to look after herself...'

'I know but...'

'Well, as things worked out she did manage, no thanks to him, nor that big ape she goes out with now...'

'Oh, Sharon!'

'...but things could have worked out better, if he'd stayed put. I know she's not perfect, but she's our mam.'

'Somebody talking about me?' Their mum walked in, towelling her hair dry. Both girls looked uncomfortable, but she didn't pursue it, because she suddenly glanced at the clock. 'Oh 'struth, is that the time? Kev'll be here any minute. Dry my hair, will you, sweetheart?'

'I can't, Mam; I've got to dash.' Sharon gathered her things together and went out quickly, before she could be delayed. 'I'm sitting at half seven and I've got to get across the park yet.'

'I'll do your hair, Mam,' said Tina.

'You'd better make a decent job of it, then. Don't make me look like one of them punks.'

Tina grinned. She had a wonderful picture of her mum with green hair and safety pins in her nose, wearing black leathers.

She loaded the hair round the brush and held the dryer close to it. She'd watched Sharon do it often enough. The smell of shampoo and drying hair reminded her of bath nights when she was younger.

Sharon had wanted to be a hairdresser in those days and had practised on them every Sunday night. She had made the whole family sit with towels round their shoulders, waiting their turn, so that the house looked like a hairdressing salon, one of those unisex places.

Tina wished they could go back to that time. Even with all the arguments, it was better than the way things were now.

'Mum, when can I come home?' she asked.

'Oh, lovey, you know we haven't the room here.'

'But have you heard any more about the flat?'

'Well, yes I have, as a matter of fact. It might be quite soon. A fella from the council came to see me this week.'

Tina stopped what she was doing and hugged her mum, catching her with a blast of hot air down her leg. 'Why didn't you tell me?' she squealed.

'Steady, you'll burn me in a minute. Now don't go getting excited. There's nothing settled yet. And anyway there's Kev to consider...' Tina looked at her mum. 'Well, we have to think about him, don't we? I mean, he's not used to kids. He might not want a ready-made family straight away. Oh, Tina, don't look at me like that. We'll have to see what happens. Everything'll sort itself out, just have a bit of patience.' Tina watched her mum's face. She looked uneasy, like a child caught out in a lie. 'Come on, love, hurry up. I've got to get my make-up on. You can watch a bit of telly until Kev comes.'

Tina sat in a daze. She couldn't concentrate on TV. She kept wondering what her mum was trying to tell her. That Kev didn't like her? The thought had never really occurred to her before. He teased her and joked with her. Surely he wouldn't do that, if he didn't like her.

When Kev arrived, a few minutes later, he said, 'Hiya, Teeny Tiny. Want another ride on my motorbike?' And he laughed, ruffling her hair. But Tina noticed that, as always, it was the same joke.

Lots of adults were like that – couldn't be bothered to find anything real to say, just trotted out the same thing every time. They seemed to think because you were only a kid you wouldn't notice. There was the old lady who lived across the street from Helen, who could never remember Tina's name. She asked her each time they met, as if she'd only recently moved in. She probably thought she was being friendly, but really she couldn't be bothered to remember.

Perhaps that's how Kev was too, not very interested. Why should he be? After all it was her mum he wanted to live with, not Tina.

'Time to go, love.' Her mum was putting on her jacket. She gave Tina a quick hug. 'I won't kiss you or I'll smudge my lipstick. See you next Friday, as usual.'

She opened the kitchen drawer and gave Tina a packet of Smarties and a couple of pound coins.

'Mum, I don't need that; my dad gives me pocket money.' She knew her mum couldn't really afford it.

'And so he ought to as well. I'm not that broke I can't give me own kid a bit of pocket money, although I know some people who'd like to think I am. There's nothing would please *some people* more.'

Tina kissed her mum and left, before she could get launched on her favourite topic again.

As she went down the path she heard Kev say, 'Come on, Doreen, hurry up; I'm sick of waiting. You know you spoil that kid. *He's* supposed to look after her. Let *him* provide the pocket money. There's no need for you to give it her twice. They have it too damned easy nowadays, kids. They don't know they're born.'

t h r e e

On the way home Tina stopped. She couldn't face going straight back to Helen's. No one would expect her until half past eight or even nine. That gave her over an hour to herself. She decided where she would go, heading off at a half-run.

She felt a little bit scared as she let herself in. She didn't often come here when it was getting dark as it was now. She reached for the torch which hung behind the door. She moved it slowly, checking everything. She could never believe that between visits no one else had found the place. Satisfied, she settled herself on a stool in the corner, leaning back on two legs, and aimed the torch towards the door. She hugged herself to keep warm.

It was a small toolshed in the back garden of a terraced house, in a row due for demolition. When she was little her grandma had lived in the next street, but her grandma and the street had both gone some time ago. These houses, vandalised and now boarded up, were the last left standing. A new estate crept closer each week and Tina knew that when the builder got round to it he'd level this row too.

But until then it was one place where she could be on her own. She could suck her thumb without anyone going on at her, even have a good cry, if that was what she needed.

Tina could see nothing wrong with crying. She wondered why the sight of tears had such a bad effect on everybody around her, and for very different reasons.

Her dad was one of those people whom it embarrassed. He looked uncomfortable if anyone started to cry and pretended not to notice. Lots of teachers were like that too – didn't want to get involved. 'Just get it cleared up' was their attitude, as if you'd spilt paint or been sick on the floor.

Her mum was the sort who couldn't let anyone cry because she found it too painful to watch. In no time she'd be in tears herself, so that Tina would have to comfort her instead.

By far the worst were those like Joanne and Helen: the button-it-up brigade, who considered it weak and pathetic. Crying, for them, was one of the seven deadly sins:

Thou shalt not cry, nor snivel nor sniff.

But for Tina a good cry was similar to spring cleaning inside her head. Afterwards she could see things more clearly, as if the tears had washed away a lot of rubbish, made some space.

The thing that she valued most about this shed was that it offered her a bit of private space.

She had discovered it back in November. Tina had been living at Helen's house for a few months by then, when she and Joanne had a particularly nasty argument. It was about whether or not Tina should be allowed to play pop music while Joanne was doing homework.

'How can I concentrate if you've got that garbage on?'

'It's not garbage. It's Kylie.'

'Exactly. Turn it off.'

For once Tina had decided to argue it out.

'I won't. You only call it garbage because *you* don't like it. You seem to think you know more than me about everything. Well, you know nothing about pop music. So just keep your opinions to yourself.'

Joanne stared at Tina for a long moment and then spat out the words, 'I wish you were DEAD! You and your stupid father, pushing in here where you're not wanted. Why don't you clear off and leave us alone?'

The shock of it hit Tina like a fist. She couldn't understand where the anger had come from. She couldn't imagine how it felt, to hate so much. And she didn't know what she'd done to make anyone feel that much hatred towards her.

The moment Dave came in, Tina begged him to let her go home to her mum. Helen and Joanne were watching them and Dave completely lost his temper.

'Once and for all,' he yelled at her, 'this is where we are living and you'd better get used to it. You're the same as your mother, as soon as there's something you don't like you try to run away from it. Well, this time you can't. So pack in the crying and stop showing me up.'

It wasn't the moment's anger, when her dad got hold of her and shook her, which upset Tina most, it was the look of disgust that followed. It was the way she remembered Dave looking at her mum once or twice, when she'd been depressed. It was a cold, indifferent look and it hurt Tina more than if he'd hit her.

She ran out of the house and disappeared down the street. As she headed across the new estate, towards her mum's house, she already realised it wasn't a good idea. Her mum would only get upset, and in the end send her back. But she had nowhere else to go.

Coming round a corner she saw two boys from school: Nick Insley and Barry Gibson. Tina's problems suddenly trebled. They were probably the last two people on earth she would ever choose to meet and this had to be the worst possible moment.

'Oh, look at the little baby,' they mocked. 'What's

the matter, little baby?'

Tina tried to walk on, but the boys blocked her path. She didn't trust herself to speak; it was certain to come out as a sob. She stayed silent, her eyes fixed on the ground.

'Somebody been upsetting you, have they? Ahhh. You tell us all about it. We're good at sorting people out, aren't we, Baz?'

'Yeah, tell Uncle Baz.'

When she wouldn't even answer, the boys began to feel foolish.

'What's the matter, cat got your tongue?'

Tina still didn't speak. She hoped they would lose interest and go away, but she knew them too well to have much expectation of this.

'Come on, we're waiting.' Nick Insley poked her with his dirty fingernail, pushing her harder and harder until she began to lose her balance. 'Careful, you might fall over.'

Barry Gibson stood by, grinning. It wasn't moral support he was required to provide, so much as an appreciative audience.

'Oh, stop it. Get off me. I hate you two,' she said, finally pushed into anger.

Nick Insley began to smile. He was always on the lookout for an excuse, the slightest provocation which he could use to justify his bullying. It gave him more satisfaction to be able to point to some small insult, or imagined slight.

Now he could say, 'Well, when she said that she was just asking for it.'

Barry Gibson, on the other hand, was equally happy with or without a reason. He was usually game for a fight any time, if somebody else was leading the way. But he wasn't keen on pushing *girls* around.

He was beginning to notice girls. He actually quite fancied one or two in his class. He was slowly winding himself up to ask one of them out. But of course he'd have died rather than admit that to Nick Insley who would have ridiculed him. So now he stood awkwardly in the background, trying not to get involved.

At last Nick Insley pushed Tina so hard that she lost her balance and fell into a garden hedge. Tina looked up into his face. He was grinning and on his cheeks were bright flushes of red. His eyes seemed lit from behind with excitement. He was a born bully. He was in fact only a few months older then she was, but he was already beginning to look like a man. His arms, thick and muscular, gripped hold of her and yanked her up.

Suddenly someone banged on a window. The boys' faces flickered with fear for a moment.

'Come on, let's go,' said Barry Gibson.

For a second, in his surprise, Nick Insley let go of Tina and she ducked away. She raced off, to make as much as she could of the small advantage she had.

She ran the length of the street, round a corner and then along a row of derelict houses. Already out of breath, she headed down the entry between two of them and found herself in one of the small back gardens. The dividing fences had disappeared for firewood; the houses themselves were boarded up. But a few yards from one of them, half buried in the long grass and weeds, was the shed. She tugged the door open, slipped inside and pulled it to behind her.

She leaned against the door, listening as the boys sped along the street and on past the end of the row, and out of hearing. She stood for several minutes, waiting for her heart to stop racing, before she even noticed her surroundings, before she realised what she had found.

After that she came regularly, mainly at weekends and holidays, bringing bits and pieces she'd begged off her mum, to make it into more of a den. Tina felt a little guilty that she'd allowed her mum to think that the things were for her bedroom. And her mum, of course, was delighted to believe that Helen was too mean to spare Tina the odd cushion or stool of her own.

Now Tina sat on the stool, in the semi-dark,

thoughtfully chewing her finger-end, thinking about what her mum had said tonight that had so unsettled her.

The only thing that had kept Tina going during these last few weeks was knowing that she would eventually go home to live. Surely her mum would be able to persuade Kev, win him round. She was always telling Tina he'd do anything for her. But what if she couldn't?

Each time the doubt popped up she shook her head, brushing the thought away, as if it was an unpleasant insect. 'Everything'll get sorted out' – that's what her mum had said. And in the meantime she just had to have a bit of patience.

Tina knew that would have been difficult for some people, they couldn't wait for anything. Helen was like that. She was always in a hurry. If Helen wanted a job doing it had to be done *now,* or preferably five minutes ago. Even if you were having a wee she seemed to expect you to stop in the middle and come running.

Sometimes Tina tried to see how slowly she could wash the pots or clean her teeth, just to get Helen mad. It was quite funny. But once or twice the look of terror on Helen's face had upset Tina, as if being late was something she seriously feared, like dying.

Joanne was impatient too. At school Tina had

watched her screw up her face and turn white with effort, desperate to squeeze the answer out before anyone else.

Sharon was no good at waiting either. When they were younger, if it was close to a birthday or Christmas, Sharon would search the whole house looking for hidden presents, on top of wardrobes or in bottom drawers. When she found them she would tear off a corner of the paper to find out what was inside.

Tina didn't have this problem; she liked to keep surprises and presents as long as possible. She loved the anticipation.

'Hurry up and open it, for goodness sake,' Sharon would say. 'Don't keep me in suspenders.'

But Tina wouldn't be hurried. She took off the paper carefully, so that she didn't spoil it, before giving her full attention to the present it held.

Tina knew how to wait. It was one of the few things she was good at. Remembering this she felt better. She left the den and went home feeling a lot happier.

four

After school, Tina lay on her bed, chewing her nails and daydreaming. She was watching Sammy climb up the side of the house which she had just made for him by cutting a hole in the side of a shoebox. With a great deal of scrabbling he managed to get onto the roof.

'Why not try the door?' she suggested.

She lifted him down and once more tried to coax him through the hole she had made. But Sammy crept away across her quilt, leaving a trail of perfectly shaped droppings behind him.

'Oh, Sammy!' She flicked them, one by one, into the waste bin.

Joanne's ears picked up the faint 'ping' and she looked up from her books. 'You're disgusting. You know very well you're not supposed to have that smelly animal on your bed.'

'Sammy's not smelly.'

'All animals are smelly, dummy, it's inevitable. They can hardly wipe their own bottoms, can they?'

Tina silently picked Sammy up and blotted him at the appropriate end with a tissue. His short legs waved helplessly while he submitted to this. Then Tina fed the hamster into the shoebox, this time blocking his exit with her hand.

Sammy began to explore and found the tissue paper which Tina had left inside for him to roll up in. Like a little machine he began to shred it, recycling it into a more suitable kind of bedding which he stored in his pouches.

'Anyway,' asked Joanne, 'who said you could have that shoebox?'

'Helen.'

'Well, she had no right to. It was mine.'

'Have it back.' Tina offered the box to Joanne.

'I don't want it now. Now that *animal* has been in it.' She used the word as if it were an insult to the hamster.

'So what are you moaning about?'

'Oh, just shut up, stupid.'

Tina smiled. These were always Joanne's last words on any subject.

There was a scratching sound of Sammy struggling to get out of the box. His now bulging cheeks were the cause of the trouble. He had filled his pouches so full that they had stretched his face out of all proportion, until his head looked as though someone rather large had sat down on it. Tina removed the lid and rescued him. She tapped him on his bottom.

'Who's a fattypuff? Hamsters who eat their beds are no better than vandals. A short, sharp shock is what you need.' And she poked him with the tip of her finger. Sammy turned round and investigated her fingernail, to see if that was worth eating too.

'Haven't you got anything better to do?' asked Joanne.

'Nope.'

'Do some homework for a change. You could certainly use it. Exercise your brain, why don't you.'

'Practise being a creep like you?'

'I'm not a creep.'

'Why else would anyone do extra maths?'

'Because I like it.'

Tina looked totally unconvinced. She stroked a long imaginary beard.

'Oh, drop off!' said Joanne. She turned back to her books.

Tina was such a drip. Joanne didn't care what she thought. She enjoyed maths because she was good at it. She found numbers straightforward and reliable, unlike people. Working through pages of maths problems made Joanne feel energetic; it was like mental jogging. They were called exercises and that's what they felt like.

Joanne could never resist trying to explain these ideas of hers. She turned back to Tina. 'Your mind needs keeping in trim the same as your body, you know.' Tina snorted. 'Your trouble is you've got a lazy brain. You let it flop around, getting fat and idle.'

This made Tina smile. She suddenly had a picture of Joanne's brain wearing shorts and designer trainers as it worked out with a few metric weights. After a cold shower it sat there, glowing with health and self-satisfaction. Her own brain, in contrast, was curled up on the bed like a large slug, dozing gently and yawning from time to time.

Tina sniggered. 'Since when were *you* interested in keep-fit?' Joanne was hopeless when she had to use her body rather than her brain. She couldn't swim or catch a ball reliably – things that most thirteen-year-olds could do. She still couldn't roller-skate without careering off the pavement and ending up in the road. Mrs Tompkins, the games teacher, called Joanne a 'walking disaster area'.

'The only part of you which ever gets any exercise is your mouth,' said Tina, 'and you never give that a rest.'

'Oh, be quiet. Trust you to miss the point. I don't know why I bother talking to you.'

'Neither do I.' Tina yawned, giving a good impression of a sleepy slug. 'Why don't you go and take a running jump? You could certainly use the exercise.'

'Just shut up, stupid.'

There was the tea-time clatter of pans in the kitchen. Helen was in from work. She called up to the girls, 'Joanne, Tina, I shall want some help with tea. Come on down.'

Tina stroked Sammy with the very tip of one finger. She sighed, and started to move.

'You heard,' snarled Joanne. 'Go on.'

'Oh, drop dead,' said Tina. She settled down again. She wouldn't go now.

Joanne turned over and began a new page. Tina scooped Sammy up and fed him yet again into the box. This time he emptied his pouches into a corner, drawing paper out like lengths of spaghetti. Then he burrowed into it, rolled himself up and fell asleep.

Tina envied Sammy. She wished she had a house entirely to herself. She wished she was small enough to creep inside his box, curl up in a corner as if she was a hamster, and disappear.

'Are you two deaf?' Helen called again.

'Coming...' Tina called back, but she still didn't move.

'Well, go on then,' said Joanne.

'Oh, get lost,' said Tina and continued to lie there, gazing into space.

Tina's complete lack of action could always be relied on to drive Joanne into a screaming fury. She wondered what Tina thought about as she lay, hour after hour, sloth-like on her bed? Nothing, absolutely nothing. Tina's head was empty. If you were to poke a pea in her ear and shake her, it would probably rattle around the empty space unhindered for hours.

Joanne dreaded the idea that people at school might connect her with Tina Parker. There were so many things about Tina she found embarrassing, not least the way she would start to cry at the drop of a hat.

Joanne would have done anything rather than let people see *her* cry. Even five years ago when her dad walked out on them Joanne had kept the tears inside. She had been used to him going away to work; he was an actor. But this time he'd written from Liverpool to tell them he wasn't coming back. Her mum said having a family had tied him down too much; it hadn't suited his image. Joanne had never really understood what that meant. But whenever she heard people talk about tall, dark, handsome strangers she pictured her dad. She still kept a photograph of him, hidden from her mum, inside her diary.

'We're better off on our own,' Helen had told Joanne. 'Don't cry over him, he's not worth it. Anyway only weak people cry and we're strong, you and me. We'll survive.'

And they had, perfectly well – until Dave arrived on the scene, with Tiny Tears, as Joanne like to call her. Since then life had been continual misery.

Joanne tried hard to concentrate on her work. Tina leaned against her pillow, sucking her thumb.

'Do you have to do that?'

'What?'

'You know very well, dimwit.'

Tina took her thumb out before she spoke and dried it on her T-shirt. 'I wasn't,' she lied.

'I could hear you.'

Joanne didn't need to turn round to check it out; it was a noise she was well used to. 'It's revolting. You sound like a baby pig.'

Tina gave few small grunts and made piggy faces at Joanne's back. 'Is it all right if I keep on breathing?'

'Do I have any choice?'

Tina didn't bother to reply.

'Don't you care that everyone at school laughs at you? I thought you were supposed to be giving it up.'

'I am.'

'Dream on,' said Joanne.

Tina lay back and sighed.

She had tried to give it up, lots of times. The trouble was she didn't always realise she was doing it; it was automatic. Some nights she lay in bed for ages, tossing and turning, afraid to put in her thumb, in case it started another row.

But the worst times were when she started missing her mum. Now, as often happened if she thought about her, Tina could feel the tears building up. She was determined not to cry in front of Joanne, so she sniffed a few times to keep them back.

'Can't we manage without the sound effects for five minutes?' Joanne turned and looked at Tina. 'Oh, what's the matter?'

'Mind your own business,' said Tina, sniffing again.

'Is mardy-bum crying for her mum?'

'Shut up! I hate you. And I hate sharing your smelly bedroom.'

'It didn't smell until you came. Now it stinks!'

Tina snatched up *The Guinness Book of Records* from by her bed and threw it at Joanne. It narrowly missed her, but swept most of her books off her desk. It landed on the floor with a loud bang:

Joanne didn't even flinch. She stared icily at Tina. 'Well, just remember – it is my bedroom. *My* bedroom, *my* house, *my* mum – and don't *you* ever forget it.'

Most of their arguments, like this one, quickly reached stalemate. They always came up against the inevitable truth: they were stuck here, both of them, whether they liked it or not.

Tina often pictured them as two goldfish swimming round the same small bowl; whichever way they turned, they could never get away from one another.

Someone had told her that a goldfish had no

memory. Seconds after it had swum past another fish it would already have forgotten. That's why you didn't really need to keep them in pairs. Tina wished *she* had no memory. She would like to be able to forget everything that had happened to her. Most of all she wished she could blot Joanne out of her brain completely, as if she'd never existed.

'Have you two died up there?' Helen's voice cut through the room. 'I'm warning you, I won't call again.'

'I'm coming,' Tina called back.

She retrieved Sammy from under her pillow, where he was burrowing. She discovered a neat hole in the sheet where the hamster had begun to make himself another set of bedding. Tina quickly covered it up and put Sammy back in his cage and went down.

Now that Tina had made the first move Joanne began very slowly to put her own things away, satisfied that she had won another small victory in the long-running battle of the bedroom.

f i v e

'Any news from school?' Dave asked the girls during tea.

He enjoyed this time of day, with everyone sitting round the table eating together, like a real family.

Joanne groaned inside. Dave talking with his mouth full always put her off her food. Here we go again, she thought. It's like an automatic response – every day he picks up his fork, lifts the food to his mouth and out it comes: Any news from school? What a bore. She carefully swallowed her own food before she answered, hoping Dave might take the hint.

Tina pretended she hadn't heard the question. She wasn't very hungry to begin with, but thinking about school usually dampened her appetite.

'We had a spelling test,' said Joanne.

'Oh yes. How do you spell parallel?' asked Dave, hoping to catch her out.

It was a great puzzle to him. Once, when Dave was a boy taking a spelling test, he had come up with fifteen different spellings of 'parallel'. He had filled half a page, leaving no room for the other questions.

And the more he had looked at it, the stranger it had seemed, until he began to think that no such word actually existed. Sometimes this still happened to him, even with quite simple words.

'One "r", two "l's", one "l",' said Joanne automatically.

'If you say so,' said Dave smiling. He could never be sure.

'They were dead easy,' said Joanne.

'I take it that means you got them all right,' said Helen.

'I got nineteen right; nobody else did. I'd have got twenty but I missed one. Mrs Bell wouldn't give it me again.'

Joanne frowned, remembering how angry it had made her at the time. She was convinced that most of the teachers had something against her.

'Don't blame Mrs Bell,' said Helen. 'You need to concentrate, then you'd get them *all* right.'

'Oh, but nineteen out of twenty...' said Dave, impressed. 'Who's a little Einstein?'

'I *was* concentrating. And, actually, Einstein was a scientist.'

'Yeah, but I bet he could spell an' all,' said Dave.

Helen caught Joanne's eye before she could reply to that. 'Yes, well, you don't know everything,' Helen reminded her.

Tina concentrated on her plate, keeping her head down to avoid being noticed. She had a way of physically trying to shrink herself during this kind of conversation, in the hope that people might forget she was there. She felt a bit like Alice in Wonderland, getting smaller and smaller. If she concentrated hard enough she might almost disappear under the table, which, in the next moment, was exactly where she wanted to be.

'*Somebody* got them all wrong,' said Joanne. She'd been carefully leading up to this. 'Mrs Bell said she despaired of her.'

There was a short silence during which Tina felt herself expanding like a balloon. She studied her shepherd's pie as though it held some important secret.

'Oh, Tina, what are we going to do with you?' said Helen.

Dave looked embarrassed, as if he'd failed the test too.

'I mean they were really easy words,' said Joanne, 'like choir.'

'Choir?' said Dave. 'Hmmm. C-h-i-o-r?'

'o-i,' said Joanne.

'Well, it's not such an easy word,' said Dave. 'Short, but easy to get wrong.' Tina watched her dad turn quite pink. 'We can't all be brain-boxes, can we?' He winked at her and Tina smiled back. Joanne hated that smile. It made Tina look like a wounded animal, pathetic, somehow naked. It always made Joanne want to slap her, really hard.

'We can't have brains *and* good looks, can we?' said Dave, slicking back his hair. 'It wouldn't be fair.'

'Oh, Dave,' said Helen, 'be serious. You don't want her to leave school illiterate.'

'Hmmm. Illiterate...now how do you spell that?'

'See what I mean? You turn everything into a joke.'

'Yeah, and that's why you love me, isn't it?' He grinned.

Helen tried not to smile, but to Joanne's disgust her mum's mouth turned up and she shook her head good-humouredly. Joanne resented the way Dave could invariably make her mum smile.

'Look, it's only a bit of practice she needs,' said Dave. 'We'll have a go after tea. You don't want to leave school a duffer like me, do you?'

Now Tina felt everyone's eyes on her. She was getting more conspicuous by the minute.

'For goodness sake, Tina, eat that food instead of playing with it,' said Helen. 'If you always let it go cold it's not surprising you don't fancy it,'

This is what happens, thought Tina, the minute they start to notice you; you can't do anything right.

'And by the look of you, I think you're due for a bath tonight, young lady.'

Three-one, thought Joanne. She could hardly believe her luck. Joanne kept a score at mealtimes. She had noticed that if Helen told Tina off, she usually managed to find fault with her too. Every day she tried to catch her mum out, but she never managed it. Today made a nice change. She leaned back in her chair to enjoy it, which turned out to be a mistake.

'Oh, Joanne, just look at your sweater. That was clean on today.' A shepherd's pie stain ran down the front of it.

'It's not my fault,' snapped Joanne.

'What do you mean, "it's not my fault"? I suppose it's mine for cooking the dinner. You say the stupidest things at times.'

'It'll wash,' said Dave. He winked at Joanne, who quickly turned away.

Three all, thought Joanne. I might have known.

Helen got up and collected the plates. 'I suppose we'd better clear this table, if you're going to play at school.'

Dave moved to an armchair and picked up the newspaper. Within minutes his eyes were closing. Too late Helen said, 'I'd have liked some help with these pots.'

Dave's eyes flickered. 'I'll be through in a minute.'

Helen sighed. 'You girls can give me a hand then.'

Joanne was furious that Dave always managed to get out of helping. This was one of his favourite methods. He'd wander in later, cheerfully offering help, when he knew perfectly well it was finished. Sometimes he'd promise Helen that he would do them later. But they'd still be sitting there at bedtime and Helen would have to do them all.

He got away with it because Helen didn't like rows. She'd rather do the job herself than fall out with him. He pretended to be helpful, but it was just a sham. Joanne could see right through him.

Tina had also noticed this about her dad and she didn't understand it. When she was little, he had done a lot of work around the house; he'd had to. Now he did nothing. Helen rattled the pots together, but it was wasted on Dave, who slept soundly throughout.

When they went back into the living room, he had slipped sideways in the chair and the newspaper had fallen to the floor, scattering itself over the rug. Tina collected it up and folded it quietly.

Although he was a big man, asleep her dad looked soft and pink and cosy. Tina was tempted to slide onto his knee and cuddle up to him. But she didn't want to wake him, and anyway she knew Helen wouldn't approve. She was thirteen now and considered too old for that kind of thing.

Tina wasn't exactly afraid of Helen, more nervous. She felt that she could never satisfy her. Helen was like Superwoman. There was nothing she couldn't do:

change plugs, put up shelves, decorate whole rooms by herself. She cooked real food, not packets and tins like Tina's mum. She had a good job; she earned more than Dave.

But Tina noticed that being good at everything didn't seem to make Helen very happy. Although Dave could usually get a smile out of her, most of the time Helen looked tired and tense. She worked too hard and she didn't know when to stop.

She walked in just then, with a pile of clothes in her arms. 'We might as well try these on now.'

Joanne scowled. 'Try what on?'

'They're some clothes from a charity shop. And there's no need for that face. Some of them look as though they've only been worn once or twice.'

It wasn't the thought of them being secondhand that bothered Joanne; it was having to dress up in them and parade around that she hated.

'I'm not trying them on down here.' She threw a withering glance at Dave, which failed to disturb his sleep.

'I don't suppose Dave would be especially interested in seeing you in your underwear,' Helen told her, 'but we can go upstairs if it'll make you happier.'

Both girls followed Helen up to her bedroom, where there was a full-length mirror.

Tina always felt uncomfortable in this room. It had

a strange, forbidding feel to it. The furniture, which was dark and old-fashioned, had belonged to Helen's father. She'd inherited it a couple of years ago, when he went to live in an old people's home. Now he was in hospital, very ill.

It seemed far too big and out of place in this little terraced house. The heavy bed nearly filled the room and it drew Tina's eye so that she found it difficult to look anywhere else. Each night her dad and Helen got into that big bed, Tina thought, and it made her face flush – imagining them lying there together. She didn't dare look at Helen; she felt sure she would read her mind.

But as usual Helen was too busy to notice. 'Come on then,' she said. 'Let's get it done. These look your size.' She threw a handful across the bed towards Joanne.

Joanne and Tina couldn't have been more different in appearance. Joanne had shot up in height very early and was head and shoulders taller than the rest of the class. She would probably end up tall and slender like Helen, but at this stage all the bits seemed to be out of proportion. The boys at school called her Baggy Baggley which was one of the milder names she had to put up with. In her clothes, Joanne sometimes looked as though she had forgotten to take out the coathanger.

'You make things worse for yourself,' Helen told her. 'When you stand like that you remind me of

Worzel Gummidge.' Joanne pulled the belt tight on a pair of black jeans, as if she was strangling someone. 'I really don't know how you do it. You've managed to make those perfectly nice trousers look like something you've slept in.' Helen loosened the belt and eased the jeans into shape.

Most of the time Joanne didn't care what she looked like. Even Dave had said you can't expect to have brains *and* beauty, and she'd far rather be clever. But there were times when she hated the way people looked at her, even her mum.

Helen always said she didn't think that girls should be preoccupied with their looks; there were more important things in life. But if it wasn't important, why did she sometimes look so disappointed in Joanne, as if she was ashamed of her? It was this gap between what they said and what their faces showed that made Joanne suspicious of adults.

She sat on the end of the bed in her underwear, chewing the flesh inside her cheeks.

'Oh, stop that,' said Helen. 'You don't know what it makes you look like.' Joanne sighed heavily.

Helen turned to Tina. 'Well, those fit perfectly,' she said. Tina was wearing a denim skirt with a cropped top. She studied herself in the mirror. She couldn't help smiling. 'Can I keep them on and show my dad?'

'As long as you don't get them dirty.'

Tina felt good. She knew she looked nice; she didn't need anyone to tell her. She'd got her mum's dark eyes and curly hair. She was a bit small for her age but that was better, she thought, than being too big. Blackpool Tower was yet another nickname the boys had given Joanne.

Tina didn't have much to do with boys. She hadn't had a boyfriend yet, but she'd received her first Valentine's card a few weeks ago, from a boy in her class. When she thought about the boy who had sent it, though, she felt almost sick with embarrassment. She hadn't told a soul about it, not even her best friend Tracey; she would have teased her. But it was a nice feeling, having had one.

Joanne watched Tina with a scowl on her face. It's all right for *her*, she thought, small and neat, like a little doll. She's got no problems; people aren't hateful to her.

Joanne could never bring herself to admit to feeling envious of Tina, 'envious of *her*', but it irritated Joanne beyond words to have to stand and watch Tina looking so pleased with herself.

As soon as Helen turned her back, Joanne mouthed, 'Nice clothes, pity about the face.'

six

When they went downstairs again Dave was just waking up. He stifled a yawn. 'Now then,' he said, 'doesn't she look a treat?'

'Mmmm,' said Helen.

'Well, *I* think she looks lovely,' insisted Dave.

'*I* thought she was going to do some spelling practice,' said Joanne.

'Oh heck, I forgot. I've got a darts match tonight,' said Dave. 'Is that the time? I'm late already. You don't really need me, do you? Joanne can be teacher.' Tina looked pleadingly at her dad. 'Come on, love, it's what you want, a bit of help. I'll see how you've done when I come in.' Then he whispered, 'You can have extra pocket money if you get 'em right.'

Helen turned away; she didn't believe in bribery.

'Have I got a clean shirt?' he asked her.

'Now how would I know?'

Dave winked at Tina and went upstairs for a wash. The girls sat down at the table, as far from each other as possible. Helen set up the ironing board in the kitchen, leaving them alone. But she left the door through to the living room open, in case an argument broke out.

Joanne handed Tina a piece of paper and a pen. Tina picked them up as if she expected them to bite her.

'Right,' said Joanne, 'one to ten. Number one...'

'Wait a minute,' said Tina. She wrote the numbers very slowly, putting off the ordeal as long as she could.

Joanne's blood began to boil, watching the slow progress. 'Hurry up, can't you. We're going to be here all night.' She picked up the evening paper and opened it as though she expected to have time to read it from cover to cover before Tina was through. At last Tina finished.

'Number one,' said Joanne, 'spell...accommodation.'

Accommodation?

Tina felt her mind go blank. It depressed her, knowing from the start that she would probably spell them all wrong. She couldn't see how yet another test was going to help her learn anything. Spelling had always been a problem to her. She wrote down what she thought a word looked like, but when she studied it she began to doubt herself. Since she was so used to being wrong, she would usually alter it, perhaps two or three times. When it was marked, she could often see that she had actually been right in the first place.

But this time she didn't even know where to start.

'I said...accommodation. Come on, for goodness sake. Can't you concentrate?'

Tina stared at the clock for inspiration. The minutes ticked by; Joanne groaned. 'All right, there's no need to look so pathetic. We'll make it a bit easier. Do you think you could manage...house?' This was worse then playing school with a four year old!

Tina wrote h-o-u-s-e, looked at it for a moment, crossed out the u and made it into a w. Joanne didn't hide her contempt; Tina changed it back.

Just then Dave came downstairs. He went into the kitchen and the steady thud of the iron stopped. Both girls turned and looked through the doorway.

They could see Dave and Helen, framed like a picture. Dave's bare back still glistened from the quick wash he'd had. Joanne hated the way he flung water around the bathroom, almost flooding the place. They watched Dave's hand stroke the back of Helen's neck. Joanne disliked his hands too. They were big, with little hairs sprouting on the backs of his fingers.

They watched Helen's shoulders, usually so tight and angular, relax and soften. Dave's head bent forward and he kissed the back of her neck. Then she turned and leaned heavily against him, her breath coming out in a long sigh, her face turned up towards his.

Tina and Joanne quickly looked away, hot with

embarrassment. Their eyes collided for a second, then darted away. Shared moments like these made them feel even more isolated.

Joanne immediately erased the picture from her mind. She was good at not allowing herself to think about unpleasant things; that way she could pretend they didn't exist.

But Tina could never leave them alone. She would keep exploring them, trying to make sense out of them. The scene had made her feel sad and lonely, and scared, without really knowing why. At that moment she wanted desperately to be miles away from here, on her own.

But Joanne dragged her back. 'Number two... caravan,' she snarled.

Caravan?

Tina tried to picture the word. She knew it started with 'car'. Her mum had lived in a caravan once, for a few weeks, when she had fallen out with Dave. It was during this time that Dave had started going out with Helen; he had met her at work. But after the weather turned cold Tina's mum had come home and Dave had agreed to stop seeing Helen, to try to make it work. Soon the arguments started up again and got worse then ever. And then it became clear that Dave hadn't stopped seeing Helen at all.

In Tina's mind the word caravan would never

conjure up a picture of happy holidays by the sea. For her it would always be associated with her mum running away.

'Oh God,' said Joanne. Tina had written c-a-r-i-v-a-n. 'What's a "carryvan" when it's at home?' Tina put a line through it. 'Number three...apartment,' said Joanne.

Apartment?

That was the same as a flat, surely, thought Tina. It was typical of Joanne to make everything more difficult for her. Well too bad, she'd had enough of this. She wrote f-l-a-t.

Joanne looked Tina in the eye and turned to complain to Helen. Just in time she remembered what was going on in there.

'Number four...bungalow,' she said in a resigned voice.

Bungalow?

Again Tina was reminded of her mum. She and Sharon lived in a tiny bungalow. They'd had to move out of their council house because they couldn't afford the rent. Tina loved that little house. It was small and compact, more like a giant doll's house really. The ceilings were low and the windows, also on the small side, let in only a little light, so that the atmosphere was always cosy, like teatime on a winter's day. And it was quiet there; most of the other bungalows housed retired people.

Tina could never understand why her mum didn't love that little house. She often moaned about it. She complained that it was damp – too cold in winter, too warm in summer – and that there was no room for the furniture. She couldn't bear living among all those old fogeys. She said it was as bad as being half way to the grave herself.

But Tina would have loved to live there with her mum, if there had been room for her. As it was she would have to wait until they got the flat. Surely her mum wouldn't go back on her promise. Panic rose in Tina at the thought.

'Number five . . .' Joanne couldn't wait any longer. 'Chalet.'

Chalet?

Tina didn't have a clue. She'd stayed in one once at a holiday camp but she didn't think she'd ever seen the word written down. It must start with s-h-, she thought; she wrote that. It was greeted by a snort from Joanne. Tina crossed it out and stared at the paper.

'Come on, thicko, concentrate,'said Joanne. 'Oh, you're so slow. Ugh! Ugh! Ugh!' She did an imitation of someone who'd had half her brain removed. 'Tina Parker, Prize Prat of the Year.'

Tina wanted to strangle Joanne. All the misery and

frustration she was feeling suddenly got the better of her. She screwed up the paper and threw it at Joanne

'Stuff your test. And stuff you. Thank goodness I won't have to put up with you much longer.'

'What do you mean?' Joanne asked.

Tina glanced nervously to the kitchen. 'Nothing,' she whispered. There was an expression of mystification on Joanne's face which almost made it worth giving away her secret, but Tina quickly regretted it. She'd kept this secret, not even telling her best friend. And for what? To let it out, in a stupid moment of temper, to her worst enemy.

'What do you mean?' Joanne asked again.

'Nothing, nothing, nothing,' Tina snarled at her, 'Forget it. Just forget it.'

But Joanne wouldn't forget it now. If Tina didn't want her to know something she wouldn't rest until she found it out.

seven

Tina alternately ate a spoonful of Weetabix and read a page of last week's *Mizz*. The Weetabix quickly turned into sludge and Tina, unable to eat it, began to stir it round the bowl.

Joanne ate as she always did, hardly noticing what was going into her mouth. All her attention was on a school exercise book, propped up against a jar of marmalade. Tina wished that she didn't care about food either; unfortunately she thought about it a lot.

Helen hurried through from the kitchen with some toast. She was eating her own breakfast on the run, while she made the girls' packed lunches.

'You've no time for reading,' she told Tina. 'And what are you so engrossed in?'

'We've got a French assessment today. I was going over it,' said Joanne, carefully watching Tina's face. She was rewarded by the look of horror which registered there.

'Did you forget again?' Helen asked.

Tina sighed in reply.

'Couldn't you have reminded her?'

'It's not my responsibility. I'm not her keeper.'

'Oh forget it! Just look after yourself as usual.'

Helen snapped the book closed, then removed it and the comic from the table. 'If you don't know it already, it's too late to be learning it now.'

'I know it,' said Joanne. 'I can't speak for other people of course.'

The Weetabix lay heavily on Tina's stomach. She wondered whether it was worth faking a period pain or a sore throat, but decided it was a waste of time in Helen's present mood. She was even more impatient with them than usual this morning.

This was because Helen was worried about her father. She'd been to visit him in hospital at the weekend and found that he was getting worse. He hadn't even seemed to know who she was. Helen hadn't said much about it, but Tina could see she was upset.

Tina went into the bathroom and sat reading the rest of her magazine. Joanne banged on the door.

'Go away. I'm on the loo.'

'...reading mags,' added Joanne.

It always enraged her, if she had to wait to get into the bathroom, to see Tina emerge quarter of an hour later clutching a magazine. Joanne thought that reading in the toilet was a disgusting habit. It was something else about Dave that irritated her.

'Well, you can just hurry up and come out,' said Joanne.

'Drop dead.'

'Are you two finished up there yet?' Helen called.

'Nearly,' Tina called back.

Tina stared in the bathroom mirror, willing herself to be sick. She stopped short of actually poking her fingers down her throat, because when it came to it she couldn't bear the feeling of throwing up. She ran the water, but then let it away. She was too miserable to be bothered with a wash.

'I'm off,' Helen called. 'And you'd better be sharp or you're going to be late. Joanne's gone already so make sure you lock up.'

Now she'd missed her chance Tina would have to see it through. She made her way unhappily to school.

Soon after the bell Tina and her friend Tracey were sitting on their desks in their formroom, waiting for registration.

'I'm dreading this test, aren't you?' Tracey asked. 'Have you learnt any of it?'

Tina shrugged her shoulders. 'Not really.'

'I hardly looked at it either.'

Tina knew Tracey was only saying this to make her feel better. She had probably been worrying about it all weekend, but Tracey hated anyone to think she was a boff. She seemed to be enjoying the nervous excitement which she always managed to work herself up to on these occasions.

'I'm scared stiff,' she said, immediately contradicting herself with a smile.

Around the classroom a few people talked about the test, while most of the others worried in private. Their French teacher, Mrs Crawdon, was a formidable person, probably the one teacher they were all genuinely afraid of.

'There's going to be real trouble for anyone who does badly this time,' Honor Walker told a group of her friends near the door. She was keen to be a teacher herself eventually. She behaved as if she was already in training, throwing her weight around and lecturing anyone who'd stand still and listen.

'Real trouble,' sneered Nick Insley, catching her full in the back with his sports bag. 'Whatd'ya suppose old Crowface can do about it? Tell us what naughty children we are? Give us lines? So what. French is a load of rubbish and Crowface is a boring old bag. I might get the whole lot wrong on purpose, just to see what she does.'

'You're all talk,' one of the others told him.

Nick Insley's response was to swing his bag again, catching the girl across the side of the head.

'Hey! Pack it in,' she yelled. Nick Insley grinned.

'Yeah, that's what we'll do, get 'em wrong on purpose,' Barry Gibson agreed.

He was one person who wouldn't have to try very hard to do that. Several people laughed. He looked round in surprise, pleased to have made a joke.

Nick Insley on the other hand could have done the test without difficulty, if he had chosen to. But he had given up on school some years ago. He had a very dark complexion and black hair and for that reason only, throughout his early school life, he had suffered from racist jokes. Gradually people had learnt better than to provoke his nasty temper, but he still carried the chip on his shoulder. It made him especially cruel to anyone darker skinned than himself and it had turned him against school for life.

Barry Gibson, or Gibbo as he was more commonly known, was his only ally. He was tall, with long arms which hung loosely by his sides. He had a wide mouth he often drew back in an embarrassed grin, and an unconscious habit of scratching himself when he was puzzled. As if to complete his image he had developed a brilliant monkey call. Breaking into this without warning during lesson time got him into a lot of trouble.

'Well, it won't be just lines or extra work this time, it'll be an after-school detention, or several,' Honor Walker reminded them, perfectly imitating Mrs Crawdon.

Detentions in themselves held no fear for Nick

Insley, but he did resent any extra time spent in what he considered the most boring dump on earth. Too late to start learning his French now, he cast around for someone to copy from.

He spotted Joanne poring over her book in the corner. Apart from ensuring he and Barry Gibson would get top marks, choosing Joanne offered him another malicious pleasure: the possibility of getting her into trouble.

Joanne's dedication to work was a constant irritation to him. Often, as he looked around the room for lack of something better to do, the sight of Joanne Baggley trying so hard made him unaccountably angry. Thinking about her, he would find himself automatically clenching his fists.

He stared at her for a moment, but she was totally oblivious to him, wrappped up in what she was reading. This made him even angrier. He picked up a school atlas from the bookshelf and threw it at her. It caught her on the shoulder. She looked up for a moment, furious. When she saw where it had come from she turned her back and went on reading.

'Hey, Baggy, we've got a rare treat for you. This is your lucky day. Me and Gibbo are going to sit by you next lesson so you can help us with our French.'

''Cause we're not very bright, you see,' said Barry

Gibson in a silly voice, again stating the obvious and raising a few laughs.

Joanne pointedly ignored them. She was well used to being the butt of people's jokes.

'I don't think she 'eard us,' said Nick Insley, moving across to press home his point. 'Listen to me when I'm talking to you, you scrawny stick-insect.'

He took hold of Joanne's ear and twisted it. Tina saw the look of revulsion on Joanne's face. It made her stomach turn over.

Joanne had a thing about being touched. She liked people to keep their distance, respect her space, and most of the time they did. At primary school she had hated it whenever you had to find a partner and hold hands. She was much happier at secondary school where, if you were ever required to work in pairs, it was only necessary to sit at the same desk.

Even at home Joanne avoided a lot of physical contact, and Helen was the same. When Tina and her dad were first living at Helen's, Dave had tried to ease the atmosphere by fooling around. He would grab Helen from behind in a bear hug and squeeze the breath out of her, or whisk her out of her chair and dance with her, while he sang some soppy, romantic song.

At first Helen hadn't known how to react. It looked as if it had been a long time since anyone had fooled around with her like that. She got embarrassed and pretended to be cross, but increasingly nowadays she seemed to enjoy it.

'Don't be so soft,' she would say, pushing him off, smiling, the good humour often lasting all evening.

Once or twice he'd tried the same tactics with Joanne. She'd struggled and squealed and finally in desperation clawed at him, her face white with fear and horror.

Helen had shouted, 'Leave her. Put her down. She can't stand it; look at her.'

Dave had let go of her, totally puzzled.

'She just doesn't like people touching her,' Helen tried to explain. 'Leave her, she'll come out of it.' But his good mood completely evaporated and after that Dave kept his distance.

Tina could see that same look on Joanne's face now. She wondered whether she ought to do something about it. But immediately she thought, 'Why should I? She wouldn't care, if it was me.'

Nick Insley jabbed his finger into the side of Joanne's face. 'Get it, Baggley? You're going to help us by writing the answers on a piece of paper, nice and clear, 'cos we're not very good at reading an' fings. Then pass it, careful-like, so Crowface doesn't see you, under the desk to me. Got that?' He cuffed her playfully across the ear.

Joanne opened her mouth. 'Don't touch me again,'

she snarled at him, her voice rising hysterically.

Hearing high-heeled footsteps in the corridor, Nick Insley clapped his hand over her mouth. For Joanne this was the ultimate horror. Her shrill scream forced its way through his fingers. The look of hatred she gave him penetrated even his tough skin. He saw quite clearly what somebody else honestly felt about him. In that moment he would have liked to kill her.

People had moved across the classroom, closing in around them, drawn by the prospect of trouble. But they scattered when they heard the teacher come in, anxious not to be associated with it.

'Whatever was that terrible noise?' asked Mrs Trask. She breezed in, as usual five minutes late for registration. 'What's going on? Nick Insley, Barry Gibson, what are you up to?'

'Nothing,' said Nick Insley, scowling.

'Nothing, miss,' Gibbo echoed, grinning.

'I'm sure Joanne didn't scream because you both looked at her, although I could entirely sympathise with her if she did. You invariably have that effect on me first thing on a Monday morning.'

Several people smiled and everyone got into their places, sensing the danger had passed.

'Well, if there's no real damage done, Joanne…? No blood as far as I can see?' Joanne gave the slightest shake of her head. 'Then let's get the register done, quickly please. We don't want to keep Mrs Crawdon waiting.'

The French teacher stood in the open doorway, studying her watch, a not very subtle reminder that the lesson, and the dreaded test, should have started minutes ago.

eight

Minutes later Tina sat looking at her blank piece of paper. Around her people were busy heading theirs with their names and the date; Tina wanted to delay starting as long as possible.

'There will be twenty questions in all,' said Mrs Crawdon. 'Each will be repeated twice. That should be sufficient for even the hard of hearing, so I want no questions and no interruptions. Is that quite clear?... *Numéro un...*'

Tina was never happy at school but usually it was a boring, rather than painful, experience. Tests and exams, however, were different. The tense atmosphere in the room always made her feel dizzy. There was something special about the sound of a classroom where a test was going on, like the smell in a dentist's waiting-room, instantly recognisable.

'*Numéro un... Comment vas-tu au collège?*'

In the quiet, Tina could almost hear her stomach churning. Once this dizzy feeling had started it only needed the words number one to send her into total panic. After that, the harder Tina tried to concentrate the more her mind seemed to freeze up.

'Numéro deux... Tu quittes la maison à quelle heure?'

Tina quickly scribbled an answer for number one, crossed it through and redid it. This way she missed both readings of the second question.

She looked across at Tracey whose forehead was furrowed with worry lines. She was chewing her lips and holding her pencil as though it would run off if she relaxed her grip for a moment. Her face was flushed and wide-eyed and she sat forward in her chair as if it was a race as well as a test. Tracey didn't exactly like tests, but she did enjoy the sense of occasion they created.

Across the room Tina could see Joanne at the next desk to Nick Insley. Beside him was Barry Gibson, who was making a most elaborate show of pretending to think out an answer. Tina thought what a fool he was.

She noticed Joanne's pained expression. She wondered whether this was because she was also struggling with an answer or, more likely, wrestling with the problem of whether to help those two cheat.

'Numéro trois... Tu as combien de temps pour déjeuner?'

Tina wondered what she would have done in Joanne's place. She must be terrified of being caught, but equally she would hate having to give in to those two creeps. Joanne refused to share her work with anyone; it was a rule with her.

Mrs Crawdon's voice broke again into Tina's daydream. 'Of course you're supposed to be writing the answers in French, stupid boy. What language do you think we've been studying all year? Russian? Swahili? Serbo-Croat? Just French will do. And no I will not repeat the first three questions. *Numéro quatre... Où déjeunes-tu?*'

Tina could never understand Joanne's reluctance to help other people. Why did it matter? It was only school work. She would have been happy to help anyone else, if she'd ever had the right answers. But she wouldn't want to get involved with Nick Insley or that idiot Barry Gibson. And yet she had to admit, she would have done it, just for a quiet life.

Fortunately it wasn't her problem. There were some advantages in being thick after all.

'Numéro six... Combien d'heures de télévision regardes-tu par jour?'

Reluctantly Tina dragged her brain back to the test and hurriedly filled in the last answer. On second thoughts, it would be an advantage not to be quite so thick at French.

After school, when she and Tracey sat on the park, comparing answers, Tina got a depressing picture of how badly she must have done in the test. Since she knew she couldn't spell properly in English, it came as no surprise to her that she couldn't spell in French either. Tina sighed. 'Wouldn't you love to be really clever?'

'I wouldn't want to be like Joanne.'

'Wouldn't you?'

'What's the good of being clever and having all the answers if everyone hates you?'

This quite surprised Tina. Although she supposed it must be true, she couldn't see why other people should hate Joanne. *She* had plenty of reason; Joanne was vile to her. But at school Joanne kept to herself and got on with her work.

'Surely you have to do more than that to make people hate you?'

'Oh, but it's the way she talks to people. She's so stuck up, so sure she's right all the time. She just gets on everybody's nerves.'

Tina couldn't disagree with that. She wondered if Joanne was aware of it. It couldn't be very pleasant to know nobody liked you. It must feel very lonely.

'I don't know how you stand living with her. I'd go bonkers.'

Tina agonised for a moment and then couldn't keep it to herself any longer. She'd been wanting to tell Tracey for weeks. She hoped she could trust her.

'Well, I won't have to for much longer. When my

mum and Kev get married I'm going back to live with them.'

'Honest? That's fantastic. No more B.O. Baggley. I bet you're glad about that.'

Tina smiled. Glad was such an inadequate word to describe how she felt. But she often couldn't find the words she wanted to explain her feelings. They always appeared too big to be expressed in words.

'Mmmm,' she said, the smile spreading across her face, 'you could say that.'

As Tina walked home, she dismissed the little doubts which insisted on clouding her sunny picture of the future. Instead she thought about how different life was going to be. It would be like having a completely new start.

At the moment Tina felt as if she was hanging in mid-air, waiting for something to happen. Every day went so slowly. For months now she'd felt dull and stupid. She couldn't be bothered with art and games, the only two things she enjoyed at school; nothing seemed worth the effort. It was true what Helen said – if Tina could please herself she'd lie on her bed all day doing nothing.

But even Tina could see that she couldn't go on this way indefinitely. She had to pick up her life again soon. She was fed up with waiting, she was ready to get on with it now.

'Please God, don't let it be long,' she whispered. And she dug her hands deep into her pockets and ran the rest of the way home.

nine

When Tina let herself in she was surprised to hear voices. Joanne was always home first. She walked quickly, anxious to get back to start her homework. But it was unusual for Helen to be in at this time. Tina closed the door behind her and hung her coat in the hall. She started along the corridor towards the living room, then stopped. Judging by the tone of their voices there was a bit of an argument going on.

'Oh, Joanne, don't be silly,' said Helen. 'They can't *make* you tell them the answers.'

'That's all you know.'

'Just ignore them or tell the teacher.'

'Oh, that would really give them an excuse.'

'An excuse? What for? Why would they want an excuse?'

'Because they hate me.'

'Hate you? Whatever have you done to make them hate you?'

Joanne groaned in exasperation. 'You don't have to *do* anything; Nick Insley and Barry Gibson don't need reasons.'

'If these boys are that bad why don't the rest of the class stand up to them? They can't do much to hurt you if you stick together.'

'Stick together, who with?'

'The others in the class. Tina for instance.'

'Her? She's the most useless of the lot; she'd run a mile. And anyway she hates me more than any of them.'

'Now look, Joanne, you've got to stop this. You two have got to try to get along.'

'Why? I don't need her help. I wouldn't ask her for anything. I'd die first.'

'Don't be so dramatic,' said Helen. 'You sound like your father. You've got to learn to get along with other people. There are going to be times when you need them.'

'That's not what you used to say,' Joanne snapped.

'Well, I was wrong; I can see that now.'

'Now you've got him, you mean.' Helen didn't reply. 'We managed fine, just the two of us, before *he* came...and that wimp.'

Tina felt trapped. She had started listening by accident, but having heard this much she didn't dare move in case she made a sound and gave herself away. They would think she had intentionally crept in to eavesdrop.

She thought about opening the front door, then

closing it with a bang, or creeping up to the bedroom. But that way she risked being heard on the stairs, which creaked badly.

This was what happened to people who listened outside doors: they heard things about themselves they'd rather not know. She felt very small and awkward, standing in the poorly lit hall, imagining what they'd think if they came out now and found her.

'Oh, Joanne, don't start all that again. You don't even give her a chance. It can't be easy for Tina, leaving her mum, coming to live in a strange house, having to share her dad.'

'Share her dad!' Joanne almost spat the words out. 'Who with? Not me. She can have him. I wouldn't touch *him* with a barge pole.'

'I don't want to hear any more. As if I haven't got enough on my mind with what's happened today, without you starting this row. I've got a splitting headache. I can't cope with this bad atmosphere all the time. You don't try to get on with them.' Helen's voice was getting higher and a note of desperation was creeping in.

'Well, I get headaches too, you know. I've got problems; nobody cares about me. I'm supposed to make an effort but who makes an effort for me?' Joanne was getting hysterical. She sounded ridiculous.

Tina couldn't bear to listen to any more, neither could Helen.

'That's enough! You're a stupid, selfish child and I'm sick of you.' Tina heard Helen's hand come down heavily on the table. She felt it as if it was a personal blow.

She started moving along the corridor to make a getaway. Just then the door flew back and Joanne came out. She stopped for a split second seeing Tina, frozen like a statue, guilt and embarrassment written on her face.

Joanne's own face turned white and drew back into a spiteful mask but she didn't speak. She pushed past Tina, flew up the stairs and into the bedroom, banging the door so that the vibrations ran through the house.

Tina was relieved not to have been given away. She counted quickly to ten, opened the front door and closed it with a bang. Then she walked into the kitchen trying to look innocent.

'You're home early,' she said.

Helen kept her back to Tina. 'I've been at the hospital.'

'Oh.'

'My father's getting worse. They rang me at work. I've got to go back this evening. They don't expect him to last much longer.'

'Oh dear.' After an awkward silence she asked,

'Can I do anything to help?'

'You can peel the potatoes, please. It makes a nice change to be asked.'

They worked together for a while without talking. It wasn't a job Tina was very good at, but she persevered. Tina felt sorry for Helen. Knowing her. father was going to die soon must make Helen very sad. She wondered how she would feel if her own dad were going to die. She could hardly imagine it; he was so big and fit and well.

She tried to picture him, a weak old man lying in a hospital bed, having to be looked after like a child. It was a very depressing picture.

'What's all this trouble at school?' Helen asked, abruptly breaking in on Tina's thoughts.

'What trouble?' Tina was genuinely surprised.

Helen sighed. It was exactly the response she'd come to expect from Tina. Even asking Tina for the time was like trying to prise something out of a shell.

'These boys that are bullying Joanne.'

'Oh them.'

'For goodness sake. What's it about? What kind of boys are they?'

Tina shrugged. 'Bullies,' she said.

'But doesn't anyone stand up to them?'

Tina shrugged again. Helen sighed and gave up on the conversation. Perhaps Joanne had a point – Tina wasn't the most helpful of people.

'By the way,' Helen suddenly remembered, 'there was a phone message from your mum. She wants you to go round tomorrow after school.'

'But it's not Friday. Is something wrong?'

'Now how would I know, Tina? You know your mum never likes talking to me. All she said was, she had something to tell you. It must be important if it won't wait a couple of days.'

Tina went red. Her heart began to race with excitement. It could only be one thing. Her mum must have heard from the council. Tina tried hard to cover up what she was feeling. Whatever would Helen think if she knew how excited Tina was at the prospect of leaving this house for ever?

'Is that OK, then?' asked Helen. 'You don't look very pleased.'

'Oh yeah,' said Tina. 'It's all right. I don't mind.'

She finished peeling the potatoes. Pleased? she thought and laughed to herself. Pleased? It was the best news she'd had for ages.

t e n

Tina and Tracey sat on a bench by the biology pond. They opened their packed lunches.

'Ugh!' said Tina. 'Look at this: a crusty brown cob with Marmite, a sesame bar and an orange.' She closed it again.

'Yuk!' said Tracey, sympathising with her.

'My mum used to give me smashing lunches: white sliced sandwiches with chocolate spread, a bag of crisps, a bar of chocolate and a can of Coke. I can just imagine Helen's face if I asked *her* for a dinner like that.'

'Why don't you? I would.'

'It's not worth it,' said Tina.

To keep the peace she took what she was given each day, usually dropping most of it into the litter bin at the end of dinner break. She took care nowadays to empty out the food and take home the wrappings, otherwise Helen became suspicious.

She didn't really trust Tina, ever since the day Joanne had seen her do it, retrieved the food and taken it home as evidence. Helen had given her a lecture on starvation in the Third World, which had left Tina feeling as if she was solely responsible for the problem. She had secretly put her pocket money in the Oxfam box in the kitchen for a whole month after that. She still couldn't make herself eat the food; she was just more careful now about being caught.

'I shall get something nice for tea anyway,' she told Tracey. 'I'm going to my mum's.'

'But it's Wednesday.'

'I know that. She rang up to ask me to go tonight. I think she's going to tell me she's got the flat.'

'When's she getting married?'

'Dunno. Quite soon, she thinks.'

'You are lucky. I'd give anything to be a bridesmaid. Fat chance though.' With neither a sister nor a single girl cousin in her family it did seem a vain hope.

'You never know, perhaps *your* mum and dad'll split one day.'

This seemed to Tracey a rather drastic way of fulfilling her ambition to wear a long satin dress. She laughed at the idea of it. 'Pigs might fly,' she said. 'My mum and dad are too old for that romantic bit. I can't imagine them split up; they're like a pair of matching armchairs.' The description suited them so well it made both girls laugh.

At least Tracey could share in Tina's excitement. 'What colour do you fancy for your dress?' she asked.

'Something pink and shiny, edged in tiny flowers, with a matching headdress and one of those posy things with a long spray at the front.' Tina imagined the wedding like a fairytale happy ending to the last dreadful couple of years. The sun would shine all day and from then on it always would.

But out of the blue that same obstinate cloud passed over, as it had at odd moments throughout the week. She pushed it away again, before it managed to spoil the whole picture.

'I bet you can't wait,' said Tracey.

Although Tina knew what Tracey meant, anticipating it was half the pleasure. Often when she went round to her mum's they talked about it for hours. Her mum regretted not having a proper wedding the first time. Now she was determined to have a long dress and flowers and a big wedding car. She wanted a daytime reception at the club and a party in the evening with a disco. *And*, even if she had to pay for it herself, a honeymoon in Spain.

Tina loved those conversations, seeing her mum happy.

'Well, I won't have to wait much longer,' she said.

It was nearly time for the bell, so the girls picked up their bags and began to move inside. The rest of the class were drifting in too.

'Oh no, we'll get our tests back this afternoon,' said

Tracey, shaking with mock fear. 'I'm sure I'll have got most of them wrong.'

Tina shrugged. What was the point of worrying about it now?

'I worked so hard as well,' said Tracey. 'There's no justice.' She sounded just like her mum.

'Mmmm, I know,' said Tina, for something to say.

'What do you mean?' sneered Joanne, coming up behind them. '*You* didn't work hard. You never do any revision; you don't get decent marks – where's the injustice in that?'

'Who asked *you* to interfere in *our* conversation?' Tracey asked.

Nick Insley, who had been quietly occupied scratching his initials onto someone else's dinner box, looked up.

In normal circumstances he was unlikely to be found protecting anyone else's interests, but if there was an opportunity for stirring up trouble, he played defender of the weak as if it was his natural role. Without a trace of irony, he said, 'You know your trouble, Baggley, you're a bully. Why don't you stop picking on people? That's no way to speak to your sister.'

'She's not my sister and you know it,' Joanne snapped.

'You live together, don't you, in the same house, same family, same mum and dad?'

'That doesn't make us sisters.'

'Course it does...stepsisters.'

Joanne didn't answer. But it was already too late. She'd foolishly allowed him to draw her into an argument. If she continued along this line they'd soon get on to the fact that her mum and Dave weren't married. Then there'd be all the usual cracks about living in sin and sleeping around and she'd be warned about turning into a tart like her mother. She wouldn't mind but half the people in the class were in similar situations at home, though that wouldn't stop them joining in jokes at Joanne's expense. Nick Insley too was hardly in a position to throw stones, but recently his mum had married the man she'd been living with. He seemed to think this now gave him the right to be nasty to everyone else on the subject.

'So...you shouldn't treat your *step*sister like that.' He grabbed Tina by the arm and dragged her over to face Joanne. 'Come on, kiss and make up.'

Their noses were nearly touching and Tina could feel Joanne's breath on her face. Tina had an empty feeling in her stomach that had nothing to do with her lack of lunch. She concentrated on making herself as still and inconspicuous as possible.

There was a most unpleasant atmosphere in the room; people were crowding round to see what Joanne would do. She stared back at Nick Insley defiantly and refused to look at Tina. In response he tightened his grip on Tina's arm.

'Don't,' she said, pulling away, 'you're hurting me.'

'Stop it,' said Tracey, plucking at his sleeve. He swung his arm back, sending her flying into the edge of a desk.

'Why don't you leave her alone?' one or two others added, half-heartedly.

'I'm just going to make The Bag apologise,' he said. 'Go on, apologise to your *sister.*'

'She doesn't have to apologise,' said Tina. 'I don't care.'

'Oh, but we care, don't we, Baz?' he said, trying to draw in Barry Gibson for a bit of moral support.

He was lounging on a desk, not paying much attention 'Yeah, we care a lot,' he said, without conviction. He didn't really want to get drawn in. While he didn't mind having a go at Baggy Baggley, he couldn't see why Nick Insley had to drag Tina into it. He had been busy carving his initials on the leg of his desk, surrounding them with a heart. He had been about to add Tina's name but, under the circumstances, he thought better of it.

'She gets too much of her own way, for our liking,' said Nick Insley. 'Now, *say sorry,*' he said in a girlish voice.

Joanne stubbornly refused to speak. Tina's arm was

aching, where his fingers were pressing into her soft upper arm. Why couldn't Joanne just say it and get it over with, anything to end this stupid, hateful scene.

Joanne's face, set like a mask, didn't move, but Tina could see the muscles in her cheek tighten as she clenched her teeth. Nick Insley began to grin. His lips drew back showing his own teeth, which were rather yellow. Then he pursed up his lips in a mock kiss aimed at Joanne. 'Mmmmm.'

'God, you'd have to be brave,' said Barry Gibson.

'Or blind,' said Nick Insley. He closed his eyes and brought his face closer to Joanne's, pushing his lips out further, searching for her face.

Suddenly, without warning, Joanne's free hand came up in the air and slammed into the side of Nick Insley's jaw, catching him off balance. The crack sounded as though she must have broken half his teeth.

For a full second he looked stunned, then he wheeled round to hit her back. Again she caught him off balance and sent him flying backwards between two desks. She ducked away and was out of the door before he could get up.

He raced after her, knocking people out of his path, but he stopped in the doorway as he saw the teacher coming down the corridor towards him. By now everyone else had heard her and shot into their places, distancing themselves from the fight which they thought might still erupt.

Nick Insley moved deliberately slower than most, a selfconscious smile on his face, but even he was in place by the time the teacher walked in.

She was calling back down the corridor to Joanne, 'The minute afternoon school starts is hardly the best time to be going to the toilet, Joanne. Be very quick, please.'

Late as usual, Mrs Trask did the register in record time, hardly noticing the tense atmosphere in the room, or the twenty pairs of eyes which turned to watch Nick Insley as Joanne walked back in.

His face never flickered from the fixed smile he'd adopted and his head moved in a nervy, continuous nod. It was quite clear that he wouldn't be able to relax until he had made Joanne regret what she'd done. She'd embarrassed him in front of the whole class. But he would rather lie down and die than show that he cared.

He kept on smiling, thinking to himself, Nobody, least of all a girl, hits Nick Insley and gets away with it. This time you've really asked for it, Baggley, and you're going to get it.

eleven

By the end of the afternoon, after a double dose of Mr Saunders droning on about their local survey and traffic census results, most people were close to sleep. They sprawled across their desks, which seemed the next best thing to actually crawling on top of them and nodding off. Their faces were pink and docile, all rebellion smothered in a warm blanket of boredom.

On Tuesdays they spent the entire timetable in the same classroom, without even the usual five minute room changes to give them a chance to yawn and stretch. Now they shifted on their chairs to ease the numbness in their bottoms as well as their brains.

When Mrs Crawdon walked in for the last lesson she hardly needed to look round to find a remedy. The air had a used, shop-soiled smell. She strode towards the windows and threw them open. The sudden draught of cold air made some people shiver and feel sick and disorientated.

'Sit up, for goodness sake,' she demanded. 'We have a lot to do in the next hour. And some of us will have a lot more to do after that.' She looked pointedly at

Nick Insley and Barry Gibson. 'We'll start by giving back your test papers.' She walked around the room handing them out, talking as she went along. 'A few surprises, but in the main rather better than last time, and closer to what I'd expected. The omission of an accent or two deprived Joanne of full marks, yet she was still clear of the next person by several points. Well done. At the opposite extreme Nick Insley and Barry Gibson got a record nil per cent.' There was a ripple of laughter which the teacher soon silenced. 'They will be spending a little time after school explaining to me how they both managed to get every question wrong and yet contrived to have identical answers. I'm sure they would agree this is quite an achievement.'

Barry Gibson broke into a grin, the irony wasted on him, until he saw Nick Insley's face and realised they had nothing to smile about.

Mrs. Crawdon hardly drew breath for the next five minutes, going through the tests and results. Nick Insley's face, which at first registered disbelief, suddenly changed as realisation dawned on him. Throughout the rest of the lesson, his eyes kept returning to Joanne, while she looked anywhere rather than at him.

Barry Gibson's face was a picture of incomprehension. If they had got their answers from the cleverest person in the class, and she'd got them all right, how was it they'd got them all wrong? He kept looking sideways at Nick Insley hoping he might have the answer, but he couldn't seem to catch his eye. It was fixed on Joanne Baggley. Barry Gibson stared at her too. Perhaps she knew what was going on. He just wished somebody would tell him.

At the first opportunity he leaned across and said, 'I don't get it. D'you think Crowface made a mistake?'

Nick Insley replied, 'It's that bitch Baggley made the mistake, the biggest mistake she ever made. You wait. The lesson *we're* going to teach *her* won't be in French.'

Tina couldn't quite take in it either; she was more concerned for herself right now. She was dreading the moment when she got her own paper back. The kind of mood Mrs Crawdon was evidently in made Tina more apprehensive. Nearly all the papers had been returned and still she sat there. But at last Mrs Crawdon said, 'Tina Parker, I think you had better come here and have a word with me.'

Tina rose from her chair and approached the teacher. Mrs Crawdon evidently thought that by having her out at the front, rather than dressing her down across the room, she was sparing Tina some humiliation. It couldn't have been further from the truth. This way the whole class would watch, straining forward to catch every word.

'Tina, I don't know what we're going to do with

you. Even the ones you got right you crossed out and wrote some rubbish instead.' The teacher affected a sympathetic tone of voice which made Tina feel more uneasy. 'This is worse then your first test. Did you do any revision at all?'

Tina avoided the teacher's eye and studied a point on the wall to the left of her ear. She shrugged her shoulders.

'Now, Tina, I know you are having some difficulties at home, but you can't expect to make an improvement if you don't try, can you?' Tina shrugged again. Her silence was beginning to anger the teacher. 'Can you?' Tina shook her head and looked down. 'I know you, Tina. You think because you're quiet no one will notice you. Well, I can tell you that tactic will not work with me.'

As the teacher's voice began to rise Tina adopted one of her survival techniques.

Quite often when teachers thought you were being intentionally stupid, they spoke louder, as people do with foreigners. They repeated exactly the same words over and over, as if they thought you were deaf as well as stupid. So in defence Tina became deaf. She closed her ears. Then, however much they went on at her, it was as if they were miming.

Eventually they always got tired and gave up on her. Even Mrs Crawdon only had so much energy to waste.

'Well?' she asked.

Tina looked directly at her for the first time, with an enquiring expression. 'Well...what?' it plainly said.

'Oh, go and sit down, child. It's like talking to a blank wall. But don't think this is the end of the matter; I shall speak to you again.'

Tina turned back to her place. She found Barry Gibson watching her, with that stupid grin on his face. She tried to stare him out, but this only made him grin wider in triumph, as if she'd given him some real encouragement.

Out of the corner of her eye Tina saw Joanne's face. For once there was no gloating smile there. In fact Joanne had hardly noticed Tina's little ordeal. She evidently had more pressing things on her mind. She was counting the minutes to home time and planning a fast getaway.

t w e l v e

Tina left school soon after the bell, walking part of the way with Tracey. They watched Joanne, well ahead of them, almost running out of the school gates.

'Just look at her,' said Tracey. 'There's no need for her to break her neck. She knows they'll be stuck with Crawdon for hours yet.'

'Mmmm,' said Tina. But in Joanne's place, she probably wouldn't have taken any chances either. Joanne was in real trouble; Tina didn't envy her in the least.

'Slapping Nick Insley, like that...in front of the class,' said Tracey, 'and those test results...she's gotta be a lunatic.'

'I wonder what they'll do?' said Tina.

'I wouldn't want to be her tomorrow,' said Tracey. 'She must have some kind of death wish.'

The shock of it had certainly woken everyone from their end of the afternoon doze. After the bell people had crowded round Joanne in the cloakroom, anxious not to miss any of the drama. They were like those awful people who watch blood sports, thought Tina, determined to be in at the kill. She left Tracey and hurried on to her mum's house, glad to distance herself from the whole business.

When she arrived, Tina was surprised to find the door already unlocked. She walked in and discovered her mum asleep on the sofa. She stood for a moment watching her, uncertain whether to wake her. Her mum looked pale and thin. She seemed much older.

This surprised Tina. Unlike Tracey, she thought of her parents, particularly her mum, as still young. Her mum often shared clothes and make-up with Sharon; she knew about pop records. She wasn't like other people's mums, nagging and finding fault with her, trying to wrap her up in cotton-wool.

Tina's mum didn't fuss about little things, in the way that Helen did. The only thing her mum cared about was having a good time and looking nice. Tina was pleased that when friends from school first saw her mum they'd say, 'Hey, your mum's cool, isn't she?'

Of course this wasn't always true – when her mum was feeling depressed she didn't care about anything. Sometimes she wouldn't bother washing her hair or changing her clothes; she wouldn't get dressed all day. She'd sit in her nightdress on the sofa, watching television and smoking. And she'd cry a lot; it upset Tina to see her. She was glad it didn't happen so much these days.

Looking at her now, asleep and peaceful, Tina felt a sort of ache. She wanted to put her arms round her mum and hold her really tight.

Just then her mum opened her eyes. 'Oh my God, you frit me to death. Creeping in like that...you could have been a burglar or a rapist or something.'

Tina smiled. 'Why aren't you at work? What's the matter?'

'Oh, I've been off colour for a couple of weeks. Couldn't fancy anything to eat, feeling sick all the time. And I'm that tired I can't seem to drag myself out of bed in a morning. I keep wanting to drop off to sleep.'

'Have you been to the doctor?'

'Yeah, I went yesterday. Although I hardly need to have bothered.'

'So what's wrong?'

'Oh, there's nothing wrong – according to him. But he's a fella, isn't he? What would they know about it? God, if it happened to them...oh, then it'd be a different story...'

Tina listened while her mum went on, getting angrier and more indignant. It was one of those puzzling conversations where her mum seemed to be saying things which Tina thought she ought to understand, but couldn't quite penetrate. Her face must have showed this and at last her mum noticed. She smiled at Tina.

'I'm having a baby, you soft thing. I'm pregnant. Haven't you ever heard of morning sickness?'

Tina's mind struggled to take in what her mum was saying. It was as if the room had suddenly got bigger and her words were echoing around it, bouncing off the walls. She couldn't seem to concentrate. It was so unexpected. Tina needed time to take it in, think it over, but her mum was talking non-stop.

Tina was thinking about babies: sweet little pink things in matinee coats and bootees. It would be *her* sister, or brother perhaps, hopefully sister. She'd look after it, take it for walks, change its nappy, feed it. A baby! Tina couldn't believe it.

But then she thought of her mum and Kev, living together with the baby. They'd be a proper family. Would they still want her? Would she be in the way? She couldn't tell whether it was good news or bad. Surely a baby couldn't be *bad* news?

Her mum's face was tired and irritable. She was talking about this baby as if it was a bit of a nuisance, a piece of bad luck, like scraping the car or losing her purse, something she'd have preferred not to have happened. Tina didn't know what to think.

'Well, say something then,' said her mum. 'Congratulations...oh goody...that's nice – something.'

'What will you call it?'

'Oh, for heaven's sake, I dunno. I haven't even

thought about it. I've hardly had time to get used to the idea yet. It'll depend...whether it's a boy or girl. Perhaps...Clint.' Her mum had always had a passion for Clint Eastwood. 'Or Kevin. It's nice to name a boy after his dad.'

'What if it's a girl?'

'No, this time it's going to be a boy; I've got a feeling. I always wanted a boy.' This thought made her mum smile. It didn't seem to occur to her that it might upset Tina.

'Is Kev pleased?'

Her mum's expression changed. She found herself a cigarette in her pocket. It was slightly squashed. She spent some moments smoothing it out. Tina hoped her mum wouldn't go on smoking, now that she was going to have a baby. She didn't think this was the time to mention it, though.

'He'll be all right when he gets used to the idea,' she said at last. 'He's not keen on kids. I mean he doesn't mind them but...he's not keen.'

'He'll feel different now it's his own...perhaps,' said Tina.

It was the 'perhaps' which seemed to upset her mum. It probably echoed her own doubts and worries.

'What if he doesn't? Oh, Tina, however would I manage, on my own?'

Tina could see her mum was going to cry. She went to sit by her on the sofa. She patted her shoulder, which seemed to be all the encouragement her mum needed.

'I didn't want this to happen,' she sobbed. 'I really didn't. I wanted to have a proper wedding, and get a place to live and have it sorted, just the two of us for a while.' Her mum didn't look up to notice the effect of these words on Tina. 'Now it's all spoiled. It'll be like last time, babies and nappies and scrimping and saving and broken nights, no chance to enjoy yourself.'

Tina felt thoroughly depressed by this picture of domestic misery. 'Is it really that bad?'

'No, I suppose not, but it's hard work. And I've been through all that. I wanted something for myself for a change. And Kev isn't going to like it. He won't want to settle down with a baby. He'll still be off out every night and I'll be in on my own. He won't lift a finger to help. He's worse than your dad, at least he knew what a tea-towel was for.'

Tina certainly agreed with that. While she didn't have anything definite against Kev, he wasn't a patch on her dad. She felt sure her dad would be great with babies. She imagined them all back together again, with a baby to make a fuss of. It was a lovely picture.

'Couldn't you *ever* get back with Dad?'

'Oh, don't be stupid, love. Now I'm having Kev's baby that's out of the question. I've just got to make the best of it and hang onto Kev. I could end up on my own with this baby if I'm not careful. I couldn't bear that, Tina.'

Tina hugged her mum's arm. 'But you wouldn't be on your own; you've got me and Sharon. I could come back here and help you. Helen and Joanne managed. You wouldn't need Kev, you'd have us, Mum.'

'Oh, Tina. Sharon's got no time for me,' her mum said, gently shaking her off. 'She's got her own life to lead. You will have soon as well. A couple of years and you'll have a boyfriend and a job too, you won't want me then.'

Tina couldn't believe this. She would always want her mum, and Dave for that matter. But she could see that this wouldn't satisfy her mum. She needed another adult and it had to be a man, even if he wasn't totally reliable, even if he didn't look like Clint Eastwood, as long as she had someone.

Being left on her own was probably her mum's greatest fear. She seemed to need company all the time. When they were younger, their mum could never leave them in peace, to read on their beds or get involved in a TV programme. She'd pester them to come down or distract them with endless conversation. Even when she took up yoga and practised her exercises every night, she did them in the living room, waving her legs in the air, while Tina and Sharon tried to see past them to watch *Top of the Pops* or *Eastenders*.

Tina could recognise this side of her mum but she didn't entirely understand it, because she didn't feel it herself. She didn't *need* people. The thought suddenly struck Tina that this was one way in which she and Joanne were alike. They had spent the best part of a year forced into very close contact and yet they had managed to keep entirely to themselves. And they could both do that because they had this solitary streak in common. Neither of them *needed* anybody else. She had always thought Joanne was the difficult one. But now Tina realised she hadn't tried very hard either.

'Will you want any tea, love?' her mum asked half-heartedly. 'There's not much in the cupboard; I haven't been out, with not feeling well. You could slip out and get a bit of shopping.'

'I'll go now. What do you want?' said Tina.

'Anything, you decide. It's just for a couple of days until I feel a bit better. I'm hoping to get into work before the end of the week. They'll be shorthanded if I don't, it's so busy Fridays.'

'Shall I make you a cup of tea before I go?' Tina didn't like to leave her mum feeling depressed.

'Not for me, love. I can't seem to keep it down. I'll ring Kev later, see whether he's coming round tonight. Try and be quick; Sharon'll be in soon. There'll be a row if there's nothing for her tea. It mades no odds to her that I'm feeling bad. She's not sympathetic like you and me. She's very hard is Sharon, takes after her dad.'

The mention of his name made Tina wonder what her dad would have to say about this news. Her mum was right, he was unlikely to be very sympathetic. She certainly didn't look forward to being the one who had to tell him.

thirteen

Tina walked down the road swinging the shopping bag against her legs. It felt like old times, going on errands for her mum. She'd always been good at shopping. She wondered how it was that from five years old she could memorise ten or twelve items without a list and yet at thirteen couldn't seem to remember even important things.

As she walked along she saw a woman pushing a toddler in a buggy and thought again about her mum's news. It certainly wasn't the news she had been expecting.

The uncomfortable idea popped into her head that this must mean her mum and Kev had been sleeping together. It was something she usually tried not to think about. It made her feel a bit hot and she unbuttoned her jacket and threw it open to the cool air. Tina wondered if Tracey felt as embarrassed, at the thought of her parents together – doing it! Or was she the only one that thought about these things? It seemed so impossible to imagine – her mum and dad – now her mum and Kev – her dad and

Helen – they were all doing it.

She wondered whether she would have felt better about it if her mum and Kev were married. Did it matter, as long as they were by the time the baby was born? Would it stop people using that horrid name Nick Insley was always calling everybody – bastard! It made her angry to think that a baby could be blamed for something that happened even before it was born. For goodness sake, no one asked to be born, did they?

You shouldn't have to pay for your parents' mistakes. Look at how she'd been forced to leave her home and move in with almost complete strangers, just because her parents fell out. No one had asked *her* what *she* wanted. For the second time that day she felt some sympathy with Joanne; she had no choice either.

Tina was so angry she stood in the road wanting to scream, throw something, hit somebody. She would have loved to throw a brick through somebody's window. Perhaps then everyone would see how she felt. But Tina could never do anything like that. She couldn't help imagining the people who lived there and what they would feel. It wasn't *their* fault.

If only there was *someone* to blame. Her mum? Her dad? She didn't really blame them. Lots of people must get married and realise they'd made a mistake. She couldn't blame Helen either, or Kev. Tina realised that the one person she did blame was Joanne, but that was stupid. It wasn't Joanne's fault.

Deep inside, Tina felt sure that it must be *someone's* fault. And finally it occurred to her. There was no one else left to blame – except herself. She couldn't think of any particular thing she'd done, but she couldn't let go of the feeling that somehow she'd been the cause of it all, that perhaps none of this would have happened, if it hadn't been for her.

It was only a vague feeling at first but once she recognised it, it seemed to settle on her like a heavy weight, slowing her down.

She noticed the time and had to force herself to get the shopping and go back. By now Sharon would be at home waiting for her tea. Tina went into the small supermarket across the road, grateful that no one here knew her and would try to chat to her. She grabbed a few things without thinking about it, paid and walked quickly home.

Sharon sat in front of the television, plucking her eyebrows in a small hand-mirror.

'Ouch! That hurt. Hiya little 'un. Where've you been?'

'Shopping. Mum wasn't feeling...' Tina trailed off. She supposed Sharon must know about their mum, but she couldn't begin to guess what she would think about it.

'You've heard the good news, then?' said Sharon. Tina nodded.

'Where is she?'

'In her bedroom, talking to lover boy. And you needn't look so worried. It's her funeral, not yours. At least you're out of it; you won't be woken up at all hours. I shall buy myself some earplugs. Although I hope I won't still be living here by the time she has it. Have you had some tea?' Tina shook her head. 'No, well you wouldn't have been able to, would you. There's been nothing in the cupboard for days. Now *she's* off her food it doesn't occur to her that anyone else might be hungry. D'you get some eggs? Come on then, give me a hand and we'll have pancakes.'

Tina smiled. Sharon couldn't have made a better suggestion.

Pancakes had always been their favourite tea. Even at eight, it was something Sharon could make for them. First she would sit Tina at the table, where she could watch in safety, then Sharon would swirl the mixture round the pan, lift it clear of the stove and flip the pancake in the air, just high enough to fall the right side up. It always made Tina squeal with pleasure.

Before Sharon would bring the pan close enough to slide the pancake onto her plate, Tina had to lift her hands and wave them in the air, to make sure she didn't burn herself on the hot pan.

Their mum couldn't make pancakes like Sharon. She didn't have the nerve to toss them. She poked underneath with a fish slice and invariably made a hole in them. And so, of course, they never tasted the same. It was something special between Tina and Sharon and remembering it now made Tina's chest feel tight with home-sickness.

When their mum came off the phone, the air in the kitchen was smoky and rich with the smell of frying. Tina was feeling full to the point of bursting. She had been unable to pass up the opportunity to smother her pancakes with lemon juice, butter, sugar *and* syrup, without having anyone tell her how unhealthy it was.

'For crying out loud, what on earth have you been cooking in here? It's enough to make me feel sick.' Their mum quickly opened the window and the back door to clear the air.

'Oh come on, it doesn't take much these days,' Sharon calmly pointed out. 'Watching me eat a bag of crisps is sometimes enough.'

'Well, just don't expect me to wash that lot up,' said their mum, nodding towards the sink full of pots.

'When did you last wash up after me? When did you last wash up, is more to the point?'

'I'll do it,' said Tina, leaping up from the table. She could sense a full-scale row building up. But no one paid her any attention.

'Don't you talk to me like that,' said their mum, close to tears. 'I'm not well and you know it. You just try to upset me. You've got no feeling you, you're hard, like your father.'

'I am not like him,' shouted Sharon, as if this was the ultimate insult, 'and I'm not like you, thank goodness. I'm *me*! I don't take after either of you. You won't see me messing up my life the way you two have.'

'Oh, that's right, kick someone when they're down. Any normal daughter of your age would feel some sympathy for her mother, finding herself in this condition, but not you, not Miss Perfect.'

'Here we go,' sighed Sharon.

Tina steadily washed the dishes, trying not to look at either of them in case it might be taken as support by the other one. She hated these arguments and realised with surprise how glad she was not to have to listen to them any more. There were sometimes unpleasant atmospheres at Helen's house, but she and Dave never had rows.

'I'm going to get ready to go out,' Sharon announced. 'I've got better things to do than stay here and listen to this rubbish.' She went into her bedroom and banged the door behind her.

Tina's mum went through to the living room and

sat on the sofa. She dabbed her eyes from time to time and stared at the television, without really watching it.

'Can I get you a cup of tea now?' Tina asked her.

'I couldn't face it, love. But there's some tonic water in the fridge. Get me a glass, will you, and I'll have a digestive biscuit. That sometimes settles me.'

'And then I ought to be getting back,' said Tina. 'I've got some homework to do for tomorrow.'

'You don't have to go yet, do you, love? I thought you could stay and keep me company for a bit. Kev can't come tonight; he's got to work late. I thought you and me could have a nice quiet night, watching the telly together. I've got some chocolate in the drawer.'

'Well, I should get this homework done.'

'I don't know. You've changed, you have, since you went to live with them. It doesn't do you any good, all this studying. You'll end up like that stupid Joanne.'

Tina had to smile at her mum's unusual way of looking at things. She thought that too much reading and school work made a person more dull, not less. Of course Tina realised that what her mum meant by dull and what her teachers would have understood were two quite different things.

And she had to agree with her mum: as clever as Joanne was at school, she was a very *dull* person. She had no conversation, no sense of humour. She had no idea what other people thought or felt about things, and she had no curiosity about them. Her mum was right; Joanne was quite ignorant about some things.

The thought pleased Tina; it made her feel superior for a change. She'd try to remember that the next time Joanne said to her, 'I suppose you can't help being thick. It's not your fault, is it, if you're a brainless idiot.' She ought to feel sorry for Joanne. She couldn't help being a boring, unpopular misfit – which reminded Tina that she was in no real hurry to go back there.

'Come on,' her mum coaxed her. 'Let's put the telly on.'

Tina managed, without much difficulty, to overcome her feelings of guilt about her homework. She stayed at her mum's until far too late and then had to run, panting, all the way home.

fourteen

On the way back Tina practised different excuses, in her head. Helen always worried if she or Joanne were even five minutes late. So she was surprised and relieved to see only Dave, sitting dozing in the armchair, half watching a football match.

'Hello, sweetheart,' he said, blinking to wake himself up.

'Sorry, I'm a bit late.'

'Crikey, is that the time? I must have fallen asleep.'

'Where is everyone?' The house felt strangely empty.

'Helen's at the hospital. I suppose you know her dad's dying?' Tina nodded. 'They don't expect him to last much longer, poor old devil. And Joanne's in bed. She went up soon after her mum went out. She said she wasn't feeling well.' Her dad winked at her. 'I think it was just an excuse. Although I must say, she was a bit flushed when those two boys turned up outside.'

'Which two boys?'

'I dunno, two young louts by the look of things.'

'Who were they?'

'Now how should I know?'

'But what were they like?' Tina asked impatiently.

'Oh, I get it; it was a double date was it? Well, you missed out there. That might teach you to come home earlier.'

'Don't be daft,' she said.

'Don't worry; if they're keen they'll be back.'

She didn't doubt it. Tina could guess who the two young louts might be. No wonder Joanne had gone to bed early.

'How was your mum?' As soon as he had asked, Dave looked away towards the television.

Tina struggled to think what to say. She didn't want to lie to her dad. And not telling him her mum's news seemed to her the same as lying. But she wondered whether her mum would want him to know until he had to. She also had a good idea what he would say. She felt enough loyalty to her mum to tell a white lie, for the time being.

'She's not feeling too well, a bit sick. It could be something she's eaten.'

'Very likely. She eats all the wrong things. And she smokes too much.' Tina thought he was beginning to sound like Helen. 'She hasn't got the sense to look after herself properly. She doesn't change.'

Tina hated to feel caught in the middle. What was she supposed to say when they criticised each other?

Dave saw her expression and realised this. He put his arm round her. She leaned against her dad.

'Dad, why did you and Mum get married?'

'Well, we had to get married; we'd no choice with a baby on the way. It's different now; people can please themselves.'

'Was that the only reason?'

'I suppose we must have got on at first. But we were too young, a couple of kids really. And you change as you get older. At least most people do, particularly after you've had children. But not your mum. She still couldn't seem to sort herself out. Even at six or seven Sharon used to organise her.'

Tina could remember when she was little, if she couldn't find anything she needed for school, she always went to Sharon, never her mum.

Dave went on, 'I thought having you would be bound to put things right; with two kiddies she'd have to pull herself together. I shouldn't have persuaded her. She didn't want any more. And after she had you...that's when the trouble started; she just went from bad to worse.'

Even though he hadn't told her this before, her dad's words had a sickening familiarity. In the back of her mind it was what Tina had suspected all along. She wanted him to stop, but at the same time she wanted to know the worst.

Dave had gone quiet, completely wrapped up in his own thoughts. He suddenly seemed a long way away from her, as though she couldn't actually touch him.

She felt a terrible panic inside her. It would soon be too late to ask the other big question which was continually on her mind.

'Dad, couldn't you ever get back with Mum...please?' The tears came in a second, as if they'd been lying in wait.

He sighed wearily. 'Oh, Tina, you know the answer to that. We've been through it times. We tried, honest we did, for you and Sharon more than for ourselves; it was hopeless. Now your mum's met somebody else and so have I. I want to live with Helen and that's an end of it.'

Tina hadn't meant to show what she felt about Helen but her face gave her away.

'You listen to me,' said Dave, getting quite cross. 'You've got to give Helen a chance. I know she seems a bit strict after your mum. She doesn't mean it. She's not picking on you. You must admit, she's just the same with Joanne.'

'I know that.'

'It's been very hard for her these last few years and now she finds it difficult to relax, but she's trying. She wants you to like her, honest.'

Tina didn't doubt it. It didn't make her feel any different, though. She was sick of being understanding about other people's problems. Sharon was right: why should she be made to feel sorry for the grownups around her? Surely they were supposed to be the responsible ones. Well, they certainly didn't act like it most of the time. It seemed to Tina that whatever *they* did was OK because it was covered by an excuse; there was always some explanation supposed to make it all right. She didn't want to hear any more explanations.

'I want you to think about what I've just said,' Dave went on. 'The pair of you are making life unbearable for Helen. Neither of you lift a finger to help, unless you're nagged. She can't stand the squabbling and I don't blame her. You've got to make more of an effort or else...' her dad was looking at her very seriously, weighing his words now, 'or else you could ruin everything. If you aren't careful you could mess it up for me and Helen.'

He means, like you messed it up last time, Tina thought. And her throat started to close so that she couldn't swallow. She felt ashamed of herself, as if she'd done something really wicked.

'You don't want to come between us, do you? It's up to you, love, your responsibility.'

Tina couldn't bear to look her dad in the face. There was a heavy silence between them that lasted for several minutes. Then the front door opened and they heard Helen come in and take off her coat and shoes.

Dave eased Tina off his knee. 'You get to bed now, sweetheart. And think on. I'll go and make Helen a cuppa.' He gave her a hug and kissed her. 'Goodnight,' he said.

'Goodnight, Dad.' She buried her head in his neck and went off to bed. She passed Helen in the hall.

'You're up late,' she said.

'I've been talking to my dad.'

'Well, hurry up now; you've got school in the morning.'

When Tina reached the landing she was glad to see that there was no light shining above the bedroom door. She didn't want to risk waking Joanne by putting on the lamp, so she stood for a moment beginning to undo her clothes. She heard a faint sound of crying. She couldn't quite believe her ears.

She quickly turned away from the door and went into the bathroom. She couldn't face that; she wanted nothing to do with it. She knew how miserable Joanne must be feeling but she didn't want to have to think about it. She had enough problems of her own. From now on she wasn't ever going to worry about anyone but herself.

When she couldn't delay any longer, Tina tiptoed to the bedroom and gently turned the door handle.

fifteen

The room was completely dark. The crying had stopped, but Tina could tell by Joanne's breathing that she wasn't yet asleep. Tina edged her way carefully to the bed and began to get undressed. She didn't make a sound taking off most of her clothes. Stretching across the bed to reach her nightdress, she banged her head on the top bunk as she straightened up.

'Ow!' she said, rubbing the back of her neck. The shock of it almost brought tears to her eyes, but she swallowed the cries, rather than disturb Joanne.

Too late, the bedside lamp flicked on.

'You woke me up, coming in here banging around. You deliberately woke me up.'

'I banged my head; I couldn't help it.'

'Oh, don't give me that. You waited until you knew I'd be asleep, then you came crashing in, making as much noise as you could.' This was so far from the truth it didn't seem worth a reply. 'It's typical of you,' Joanne went on, getting herself more worked up. 'You think about nobody but yourself.'

It felt good to have someone to take out her misery

on, instead of holding it inside, where it was smarting like soap in a cut.

'Oh, shut up,' said Tina. She was in no mood for this kind of rubbish.

'Likewise.'

'Anyway, you weren't asleep.'

'Oh yes I was.'

'You weren't; I heard you crying.'

'You did not! I was asleep,' Joanne insisted.

Tina couldn't be bothered to argue with her. They both knew the truth. The ridiculous lie seemed to hang in the air.

'I was asleep!' Joanne screamed at her. She clutched the quilt between her fists, as if she would squeeze the last drops of life out of it. 'I don't cry,' she said. 'Only babies cry – mardy-bums like you, crying for your mummy. Well, why don't you go back to her. I wish you would.'

'So do I!'

'Why don't you then?' It was a challenge. 'Go on, if you think she'd have you.'

Tina stood in the circle of light, half undressed. She wanted to climb straight into bed in her underwear and hide under her pillow and go to sleep, preferably for ever. Being made to admit that she was probably never going home would have been as bad as losing all hope. She couldn't bear that, not in front of this monster.

'For your information I *am* going home and quite soon.' Tina finished getting undressed. She could tell by Joanne's face she didn't believe her, but the news had silenced her. 'When my mum gets married, I'm going back home to live, for good.'

'Yeah and I've got a long pink beard,' said Joanne.

'Well, that at least would be an improvement.'

Tina brought Sammy over to the side of her bed. She climbed in and lifted the hamster out of his cage. She held him close to her face and kissed him.

'You're not going to sleep with that smelly creature in your bed.'

'Just turn the light out.' And then because it got no response Tina added, 'Please!'

Lying in the dark she again regretted saying anything to Joanne. She was worried that she might tell Helen, or her dad. Dave would have been angry if he'd even suspected how much she was banking on going home. But she couldn't bring herself to ask Joanne not to. It would only ensure that she did.

Tina thought through all that had happened that day. She didn't know what to do, who to ask for help. Her mum had enough to worry about. She couldn't talk to her dad. At one time she might have been able to talk to Sharon, but now she seemed more like one of the grown-ups, preoccupied with her own problems. And friends couldn't really help.

Tracey was OK, but she didn't understand. Her family was so different. They reminded Tina of a family in an advert. Tracey's dad was fat and jokey. Her mum didn't go out to work. She cooked steaming dinners and kept the house clean and warm, ready for the happy family to come home to. They might tease each other but they never rowed, walked out on each other, turned their backs on their kids. Oh, why couldn't her family be like that – more normal.

That wasn't right either. As soon as Tina thought about it, she realised that Tracey's wasn't the normal kind of family. In their class at least, Tracey was one of the exceptions. Most people were short of a mum or dad, or lived with somebody else's. Those families you saw on TV – they weren't real. Perhaps they had been once upon a time, but now they were like the last of the dinosaurs.

So there was no one she could talk to. It didn't enter her head to try to talk to Joanne. If it had she would have quickly dismissed the idea. Joanne's opinion was of no interest to Tina.

Above her, in the top bunk, Joanne lay struggling with her temper. She was thinking about those two imbeciles from school turning up outside her house. How dare they! What did they think they were going to do, anyway, with Dave there? Hanging about under the lamp-post across the street, as if they expected her to come out! Did they think she was stupid?

Dave had grinned at her, when he first saw them, sort of nudge, nudge, wink, wink, as if they were sharing some secret. If she had a proper dad, instead of that dimwit, she would have told him all about it. He'd have made them go away and leave her alone. But she didn't have a dad, she had Dave!

Anger filled her chest, compressing her lungs.

Joanne couldn't decide which was worse: to feel this angry or to feel this afraid. She couldn't bear those boys to touch her. It wasn't just that she was frightened of being hurt, which she was, but it was also the humiliation of other people seeing them hurt her. And knowing that some people would actually be cheering them on. She wanted to scream and shout and hit somebody, kill them actually. She fought with her tears as if they were the enemy.

Joanne hated to cry. She associated it with weak people, like Tina. Goodness knows what *she* had to cry about. Nobody had promised to beat her up. People didn't hate her and laugh at her behind her back. How could Tina begin to understand how she felt? Joanne didn't even feel she could rely on her mum any more, now that she had Dave. She wished there was just one person who would stand up for her. But people at school didn't seem to want friends with minds of their own; they preferred wimps like Tina.

Joanne heard the familiar sucking sound from below. God, how it irritated her!

'Oh, pack it in. I don't know how you can bear to do it. It makes me feel sick listening to you!'

There was no response from Tina.

It irritated Joanne when Tina refused to answer her, went silent rather than let Joanne draw her into an argument. She didn't usually have any interest in what Tina thought; but right now she'd have been glad to know what anyone else would have done in her place.

'I suppose you'd have let them push you around, wouldn't you, let them walk all over you?' Tina still refused to speak. 'Well, why should those bullies have it their own way? Someone's got to stand up to them.' There was only silence. 'Oh, it's easy for you to keep out of it. Nobody's threatening to beat you up. Go bury your head. Why should you care?'

'I don't,' said Tina. 'Go to sleep.'

Joanne turned over heavily making the bunk beds lurch. 'Thanks for nothing. I'll know not to depend on you.'

'Good.' Tina held Sammy close to her face. She thought to herself, that's right, Miss Brain of Britain, leave me out of it. You can solve this little problem for yourself.

Instead Tina concentrated on her own problems. She began thinking through the different options which were open to her now. She might be able to go home to her mum – but it looked very unlikely. She could stay with Dave and Helen – but she couldn't see how it might work. She and Joanne would never get on; that wouldn't change. In the end Dave and Helen might split up and if they did Dave wouldn't forgive her.

But if Tina wasn't here, perhaps then things might work out. Everyone else would be a lot happier. Joanne certainly would; she'd probably hang the flags out. Helen would be happier, according to Dave, and so that meant he would too. And she would be happier, herself; she couldn't be much less happy.

Running away seemed to be the obvious answer. Why hadn't she ever thought of it before? The idea came to her just as she was dozing off. She still had lots of problems but at least now she had a plan. She could start to do something, make her own decisions, instead of waiting for other people to make them for her.

She kissed Sammy lightly on the end she hoped was his nose, then put him back in his own bed, 'And don't you worry, I shall take you with me,' she whispered, almost asleep. 'I wouldn't go anywhere without you.'

sixteen

Next morning, when Tina first woke, she couldn't work out where she was. Just occasionally she still opened her eyes expecting to find herself in her own bedroom. Then the reality dawned on her and she turned over, unwilling to get up and face the day.

It seemed quite dark and Tina thought it must be early. There was no movement above her. Normally Joanne was up first, banging about, drawing back the curtains. She took out her watch and screwed up her eyes to read it. In fact they were a little later than usual.

To confirm this Helen's voice suddenly penetrated the room. 'Are you girls thinking of getting up this morning?'

'Coming,' Tina called back. The tone was meant to give the impression that she was actually on her way down. She had discovered that this was a good way to forestall Helen's nagging. But at last Helen was getting wise to it.

'Well I won't call again. D'you hear?'

'I'm coming *now*.'

Tina pulled the quilt around her. She had tossed and

turned so much in the night that it had almost slipped off the bed and she had woken up feeling cold and shivery. She heard Dave whistling as he left the house for work and immediately remembered her decision to run away.

It still seemed the best idea, but the reality of it was far more frightening this morning. She didn't know how to begin planning it. Where could she go? What should she take? How soon could she be ready? She had no answers to these or any of the other questions which crowded into her head. She could hardly bear to think about them. There was one thing Tina was sure of, that the more she thought about it the harder it would be to do. She would have to go today, or she never would manage it.

After she had warmed up a bit, Tina began to get dressed, drawing her clothes one by one from the radiator beside the bed. She pulled them under the quilt and struggled into them like someone trying to get dressed inside a bag. She went to elaborate lengths each morning to expose as little bare skin to the cold air as possible. For once Joanne wasn't able to tell her how mardy she was.

'It's late, you know,' Tina told her. She drew the curtain back.

'Don't do that,' Joanne shrieked, pulling her quilt over her head. 'I'm not well. I'm not going today.'

'What's the matter?'

'I'm ill, stupid, I just told you. I've got a headache and a stomach ache and I'm not going.'

It was unusual for Joanne to be ill and Tina was inclined to believe her. She was the one who usually tried to avoid school. But soon Tina remembered the bullying, and evidently so did Helen.

'Come on,' she said, coming in and pulling back Joanne's quilt. 'Let's have you down for breakfast, then we can see if there's anything wrong...other than a spot of skivalitis.'

'I'm not well, Mum, honest. I don't want to go today.'

'Come along, Joanne. It's no good hiding in there, trying to avoid the problem. It won't go away. It'll just have to be faced another day. If it's these boys that are bothering you, you must tell the teacher. She'll put it right. But you'll see, they'll have forgotten about it by now. Boys like that, they're all talk.'

This only confirmed for both girls how out of touch most adults were. They had little idea about the kind of ordeals you had to face daily in most big schools. There was no point trying to tell them; they always thought they knew best and you knew nothing.

Already conceding defeat, Joanne began to get dressed. Once she could see this, Helen hurried downstairs to get the lunches. She had no more time to spend on her this morning.

Helen was too busy at work and had too much to do at home. She was worrying about her father, dying in hospital. She felt guilty that she hadn't brought him home to die in peace. But how could she do that? There was no room for him. And anyway the atmosphere in this house was far from peaceful.

She was exhausted, trying to smooth things over between the girls. Her head ached with the effort of holding everything in it: all the things she had to do each day, all the things she needed to remember. She felt like one of those circus performers, attempting to keep a dozen plates spinning in the air at the same time. She tried to keep her eye on every one, terrified that if she stopped for a moment, they'd come crashing to the floor.

'Will you please hurry, just this once?' she called up again. She had hoped to get into work early, to make up for the time she'd been taking off to visit her father. Her boss was beginning to lose his patience. She rushed from one job to another, checking her watch as if she was in a race.

Tina sat down at the table and watched her. She noticed how thin Helen was getting. Her mum was right: despite her talk about health foods, healthy was the last thing Helen looked. Even her skin seemed overstretched, no more give left in it.

Tina felt partly responsible for this. She found

herself wanting to go up and put her arms round Helen, to make her stop for a minute, to get her a cup of tea. Tina thought most things could be put right with a cuddle and a cup of tea.

But suddenly Helen turned and saw Tina watching her, making no attempt to eat her breakfast or get ready for school. 'For goodness sake, can't you get on and eat something? Do you do it on purpose, to make me angry? Is that what you set out to do?'

Tina winced and bobbed her head as if Helen had hit her. She looked so hurt that Helen had to turn away. She couldn't cope with Tina's tears this morning. Getting her voice under control, she said, 'I want both you girls to hurry home from school today. I've got to visit Dad at the hospital. I want you to get the tea on. It's only a nutloaf to warm up and the veg to do. They're all out ready in the kitchen.'

Neither of the girls spoke, or in any way acknowledged her. 'Did you hear me?'

Tina nodded.

Joanne spoke slowly, barely opening her mouth. 'I'd rather do it on my own.'

'You'll do it together.'

Joanne seemed to completely disregard the danger signals. Her face was quite flushed this morning and her eyes had a wild gleam in them, like someone heading for trouble.

'I don't want to do it with *her*,' she said quietly, but clearly. 'I'll do it on my own.'

'You'll do as you're told, do you hear me?' Helen banged her fist on the table so that the cereal packets fell over, spilling their contents on the floor. Nobody moved. 'I have just about had enough of you two. You don't give an inch.' She looked at Joanne. 'You're so selfish and ill-tempered, no wonder people fall out with you. But you're no better,' she told Tina, 'ghosting about the place, looking, pathetic and put-upon. I have tried to make things easy for you and you don't even seem to notice. Well, I have had ENOUGH,' and again she banged hard to underline her words. 'You're driving me mad. I can't stand any more. Now have I got through to you both?'

Tina couldn't bear to meet Helen's eye. Joanne stared at her mother in horror. Helen snatched up her things and stormed out, leaving the mess and the lunches half-made. Within minutes she was out of the house, hurrying down the street.

The two girls refused to look at one another. Joanne said again, 'Like I said, I'll do it on my own.'

'Suits me.' Tina got up and finished making her own packed lunch. She wouldn't be here anyway. If she was serious about running away, she might as well go now. For a moment she was tempted to say to Joanne, 'Don't bother setting a place for me.' Instead she went upstairs, leaving the mess where it was for Joanne to sort out.

Once inside the bedroom she moved fast. She grabbed a rucksack and stuffed a few warm clothes into it, a pair of pyjamas and a soapbag. She stopped to think what else she might need.

Money – she had a few pound coins in her drawer, that wouldn't get her far, but it would have to do. She was starting to sort Sammy's food when she heard Joanne's feet on the stairs. She pushed the bag under the bed and pretended to be getting ready for school.

The girls didn't speak to one another. Tina soon got the feeling that Joanne was waiting for something. It made no sense, Joanne never waited for her. Then Tina remembered that Nick Insley and Barry Gibson might well be outside, waiting for Joanne.

This threw her into complete confusion. She had to get rid of her. She couldn't do anything with Joanne hanging around watching. She needed a bit of space to work out a plan.

Tina didn't intend to go to school – it seemed stupid under the circumstances. If she did she wouldn't be able to take anything with her. She'd soon give herself away carrying a hamster's cage round all day. But if she didn't go, Joanne would probably tell someone and they'd check up on her. Oh hell and damnation!

Tina moved as slowly as she could. She sensed Joanne watching her, nearly bursting with impatience. Tina disappeared into the bathroom. She sat on the toilet while she tried to think clearly.

If she could get rid of Joanne she could take her things and hide them in her den; it was on the route to school. She could leave them there, go to school, then pick them up later. She would just have time for that, provided she ran all the way.

She heard Joanne's anxious voice outside the door. 'We're going to be really late.'

'What do you mean "we"? Nobody's making *you* late. Unless of course you're scared to go on your own.'

'You go to hell.' She heard Joanne banging down the stairs and out of the door. 'And I'm leaving the key by the door, so don't forget to lock up first!'

Tina let her breath out with relief. She raced around, grabbing things: Sammy's food, a small cage, a bottle of water, her headset and a few favourite CDs and, on a sudden last impulse, photos of her mum and dad. Then she closed the bag, picked up Sammy and left the house.

She locked the door, took out the key and stood there for a moment with it in her hand. What on earth should she do with it? There was no point taking it with her. She dropped it through the letter-box. It was only as she heard it hit the floor that she thought of

Joanne and wondered how she would get into the house tonight.

Well, there was no time to think about it now. That would be a little problem for The Brain to solve.

Tina half ran along the street, struggling with two bags and a hamster cage. Sammy, bouncing from side to side, looked terrified, but she didn't dare slow down. She couldn't imagine anyone had ever run away before with so little thought and planning. At the moment her one aim was to get to school on time. She would think about the rest later.

When she reached the shed Tina hid her bag in a corner, behind a stack of wooden seed trays, and Sammy next to it. As she got up to go she felt her stomach lurch at the prospect of leaving him here unprotected. She thought she was going to be sick; she leaned her back against the wall and closed her eyes until the feeling passed off. She realised that it was herself she was really feeling afraid for.

Looking at her watch she saw that she was certainly going to be late. 'It's only for today,' she promised Sammy. She closed the door securely behind her and set off running. Soon she could hardly breathe but she didn't stop, she didn't dare. Today of all days she couldn't afford to get a detention.

seventeen

Mrs Trask looked out of the staff-room window and saw an anxious figure racing through the school gates. It caught her attention because it was such an uncommon sight – Joanne Baggley was rarely seen running anywhere. She was so awkward, all arms and legs. The teacher had once heard Joanne referred to as Olive Oyl, and there was certainly a resemblance. Although Joanne had a good brain and was prepared to use it, there was something about her which the teacher didn't like.

But then she wasn't particularly fond of the other one either. Tina Parker was too quiet and secretive; you could never tell what that child was thinking. They made a most unlikely pair. She wondered what they could possibly find to talk about when they were on their own.

A moment later another unhappy alliance ambled through the gates – Nick Insley and Barry Gibson. She could see they were enjoying a joke, no doubt at someone else's expense. Mrs Trask decided that she must have done something really wicked as a child, to deserve both of them in her form. Most of her break times were taken up listening to other staff complaining about the two boys. She wondered what they expected *her* to do. Even when she wore high heels, both boys were head and shoulders taller than her. It was a grave disadvantage to a secondary teacher, she thought, to be looked down on by most of your class.

The school bell had rung minutes ago. When she couldn't put it off any longer, she collected up her things and made her way to the formroom. She had already finished the register by the time Tina burst in. She went straight to her place without looking at the teacher. She was red and breathing heavily.

'That's all right, Tina,' said Mrs Trask, 'don't mind me; I'm only a piece of the furniture.'

Under his breath Nick Insley made a few suggestions to Barry Gibson which piece in particular.

'Sorry. I...er...I'm afraid...' Tina looked as if she might dissolve into tears if pressed.

'Oh, do sit down.' Mrs Trask preferred not to get involved. She thought there must have been trouble at home, because both girls were acting strangely this morning. She had no time to be bothered with it now. She altered the register, which was always easier than giving out detentions. 'You'd better get off to your first lesson,' she said, making a quick getaway herself.

But Tracey could hardly wait to find out what was

going on. Tina hadn't begun to get her breath back before she started firing questions at her.

'Where have you been? Why were you late? What's up with Joanne? She came in looking like a lobster on heat. Have you been falling out? What's happened about her and Nick Insley?'

Tina hardly listened; her mind was on other things. The girls were soon outside the classroom and Tracey still hadn't found out. She grabbed Tina's arm.

'Come on, don't hold out on me. Quick.'

Tina couldn't get her breath properly. She felt hot and dizzy and something inside her snapped.

'How should I know!' She jerked her arm away. 'It's nothing to do with me.'

'Don't wet yourself,' said Tracey. 'I'm sorry I asked.'

'Well, don't then.'

'Don't worry, I won't. I don't know what's the matter with you.'

'There's nothing the matter with me. It's everyone else that's the problem.'

'You're not perfect, you know. You're really hard work.'

The two girls, normally quiet and easy-going, stood in the middle of the corridor, snapping at each other, until quite a curious little crowd gathered around them.

'I don't know what you mean,' said Tina, lowering her voice.

'I mean the way you droop around the place as if the end of the world's coming. Trying to have a conversation with you sometimes...it's like trying to walk uphill with a heavy weight on your back.'

Tina couldn't be bothered to listen to any more. She went into the classroom, but Tracey followed her. Now she had started, she was determined to finish. She spoke in a loud whisper, 'You're so miserable lately. You're boring, boring, boring. You want to be careful, you know, you'll end up like Joanne.'

Unable to think of a worse insult, Tracey moved across the classroom to sit as far from Tina as she could. She looked like someone who had finally got something off her chest and felt better for it.

Falling out with Tracey seemed to exhaust Tina. The misery was choking her up inside until she could hardly breathe. She slumped down in her chair, her head on her hand. She couldn't wait for home time. She would be better off when she was completely on her own; she could cope with that. But feeling so friendless, while you were actually surrounded by people, was quite different. It felt very lonely. This must be how Joanne felt most of the time.

She spent the morning counting off the minutes, even though she knew it was the surest way of slowing down the clock. Somehow she managed to get through it and when the bell rang she realised with relief that she was halfway there.

She took her sandwiches and sat on a bench by the biology pond. She didn't bother to open them; she wasn't hungry now and she might need them later.

While there were a lot of other people around, there was no one who would pay any attention to her. Tracey had kept well clear of her all morning, which suited Tina. She was also particularly anxious to avoid Joanne, in case she asked for the key.

But Joanne was too busy avoiding the boys. At the moment they were enjoying themselves just winding her up. They were finding lots of little ways to make her suffer. They had already followed her to school, calling after her, 'Hey, sexy, wait for us.' They whistled and shouted rude remarks, amusing themselves and embarrassing her.

Now Tina saw them race round the corner from the dinner hall. They were clutching Joanne's schoolbag, and seconds later Joanne followed, grabbing the bag and struggling to get it off them.

The struggle caused a lot of interest around the pond and one or two people cheered them on. Barry Gibson wrenched Joanne's arms behind her back and held her by them, while Nick Insley opened the bag and held it over the pond.

'Don't you dare,' Joanne yelled at them.

'Are you daring us, Baggy?' asked Barry Gibson, delighted.

'Well...you asked for it.' Nick Insley tipped the bag upside down and shook the contents into the water. Then he dropped the bag in too. A few people applauded.

Barry Gibson was getting quite excited. 'What d'ya reckon we throw *her* in as well?' He pushed Joanne forward in readiness. He glanced round for some encouragement, smiling straight at Tina, as if he was offering her a special favour. She glared at him. She wished he would stop trying to be nice to her; it made her feel sick.

Tina could tell by his face that Nick Insley was tempted by the idea. But he knew they wouldn't get away with it. When his moment of revenge arrived he wanted to be able to take full advantage of it.

'Now, don't be greedy, Baz. We can wait till half past three. We'll see you after school, Baggy.'

'Don't go without us,' said Barry Gibson, miming a big kiss.

'Whoo-whoo,' mocked one or two onlookers.

The bell rang then and most people drifted off. A few had difficulty tearing themselves away. They wanted to watch Joanne get her things out of the water.

Tina hung back too. She wasn't sure why; she really didn't want to get involved. But the unpleasant way people were jeering at Joanne and enjoying her misery upset Tina.

She'd once been on the park when a group of boys had been teasing a cat. She had watched horrified as they threw stones at the poor animal which finally escaped, limping badly. She felt the same kind of disgust now.

Although the pond was only knee-deep, it was wide and Joanne was having trouble reaching her things. She knelt on the side and fished out sodden exercise books. She didn't seem to know what to do with them. Her empty dinner box and drink bottle floated away from her. Her bag had caught on a clump of water weed right in the middle. She was making a real business of it. In her place Tina would have taken her shoes off and waded in, to get it over with, but she knew Joanne wouldn't do that.

Tina was beginning to feel some of the embarrassment, as if people were laughing at her too. She wanted to shake some sense into Joanne, tell her to get on with it.

'Oh, for goodness sake...' she said.

She pulled off her shoes and socks and stepped in. Several people started to cheer. It felt slimy and unsafe underfoot. Tina tried not to think what unmentionable things might be squelching between her toes. Once or twice she nearly slipped and got wetter than she had bargained for, but in a few minutes she'd retrieved everything. There was an outburst of applause as she came out dripping, drying her hands on her skirt.

Joanne hardly looked at Tina; she didn't speak. She scooped up her things and went into school, leaving Tina to sort herself out. Tina arrived late for registration for the second time that day.

By now Joanne was too scared to report the boys. Instead she told the teacher she'd dropped her bag in the water herself, by accident. It was not an uncommon event, people were often mysteriously letting go of their things into the biology pond. Mrs Trask would have hardly been surprised at some people offering this excuse. But it was not very convincing coming from Joanne.

When Tina came in late again, her skirt wet, her legs mud-splattered, Mrs Trask put two and two together and miscalculated. 'I don't know what's going on between you girls today. If this is some silly argument from home that you're carrying on in school, you're going to find yourselves in real trouble with me.' Tina looked incredulous. 'If you think it's amusing throwing people's things into the biology pond...'

'It was nothing to do with me!' Tina shouted. It seemed so out of character it shocked everyone into silence.

'Don't you dare shout at me, Tina Parker. There

have been one or two complaints about you lately. Mrs Crawdon spoke to me only yesterday about your attitude. I'm beginning to see what she means.' Tina's face was full of contempt and it stung the teacher even further. 'You can both stay behind after school and we'll sort this out then.' She went out, leaving the whole class stunned by the injustice of teachers.

Nick Insley and Barry Gibson couldn't believe their luck. As long as he was in the clear, Nick Insley didn't mind who else took the blame. But, to his own surprise, Barry Gibson felt a new and uncomfortable sensation – he was tempted to own up.

The rest of the afternoon had a strange quality to it. It seemed to Tina to drag on relentlessly, yet at the same time there was an atmosphere of panic and excitement which made her feel as if she was being rushed towards some unpleasant climax.

Tina was determined to keep well clear of Joanne's trouble with the boys. She kept on telling herself it was nothing to do with her. And she had no intention of staying behind to see Mrs Trask; Joanne could tell her just what she liked. Tina was ready to be off the minute the bell went. They wouldn't see her for dust.

eighteen

Tina didn't stop running until she reached her den. She put her head down and ran as though her life depended upon it. She didn't allow herself to think about anything except getting there. A buzzing started up inside her head, as if a bee had crawled in through her ear, but she didn't stop. When she reached the shed she let herself in and sat panting, her eyes closed.

Now the buzzing changed to a drumming sound; her head felt about to burst. She held it between her hands because it seemed too heavy to be supported by her neck alone. Gradually the drumming slowed to a gentle pulsing. At last she could bear to open her eyes. She looked around and took in the fact that she was here, safe at last.

In daylight the shed appeared much more ordinary and shabby than in torchlight. The floor was gritty; everything was covered with cobwebs. But already the magic was working. The peace and quiet settled around her like a warm blanket. This was the nearest she came these days to being in her own place.

That was what Tina missed most of all: the feeling

that she belonged anywhere. She was like a visitor at her mum's, or an unwanted lodger at Helen's; but in this shed she felt at home.

The thought of running away seemed to have come to her a long time ago, perhaps in a dream. She wondered how she had ever seriously considered it; she was so tired she couldn't even think it through. Right now she would have liked to curl up on a sofa in front of a television and watch hours of what Helen described as mindless rubbish.

She went over to Sammy's cage and got him out. He was wrapped in a bundle of bedding. While she had endured an agonising day at school, she thought, Sammy had passed the hours peacefully sleeping.

Tina sat stroking the hamster and wondered what she could do now. She had no more idea than she'd had that morning. Perhaps she could just stay here, at least for tonight. It would give her a chance to think things out. She had only to look around her to see that she couldn't really stay for long. The shed was cold and dirty and hardly weatherproof. There was nowhere to sleep, apart from sitting on this stool; she had never slept sitting up before. There was nowhere to have a wash, although this didn't strike Tina as a problem, but she couldn't go to the toilet either. While she didn't mind weeing behind a bush, if she had to, she couldn't bear to do the other outside.

Her empty stomach also reminded her that she had very little food with her and not much money. What a stupid idiot she was. Why hadn't she thought it through properly? She could have got more money. She could have brought some blankets. Had she been organised she could have stayed here for a couple of days before anyone found her, if anybody even bothered to look. She wondered who would miss her, who would care that she'd gone.

Tina leaned back against the wall and ran a little fantasy through her head in which she played the heroine. She imagined herself in this very shed wrapped in rugs, blue with cold and weak from lack of food. She looked gaunt and hollow-eyed like the Little Matchgirl. Tina remembered her sad face from one of her picture books.

It was a small leap from there to imagining herself dead from hypothermia, her poor thin body only discovered after days of searching by policemen and teams of local volunteers.

'13-year-old from broken home starves to death in garden shed,' the headlines would say. 'Parents devastated.'

Tina was so moved by this idea that her eyes began to sting. She sniffed a couple of times. And then she moved on to the more satisfying business of imagining her family and friends eaten up with remorse and guilt.

A picture of her grief-stricken mum appeared in Tina's mind. She was just beginning to look pregnant and she was weeping on Kev's shoulder. 'I want my little girl back.'

'She's gone, love. No use crying any more,' said Kev. 'You've got the baby to think about now.' But her mum wouldn't be consoled. A single tear ran down the side of Tina's face.

Next she saw Dave, head in hands, sitting in the living room being comforted by Helen. Joanne stood in the background, sobbing. Each of them was trying to take the blame for what had happened.

'It was all my fault. I was busy thinking about myself,' said Dave, almost in tears.

'No, it was me,' Helen insisted. 'I was too hard on her.'

'No, it was me,' Joanne sobbed. 'I drove her away. It was because of me she got into trouble. It was my fault.'

Then Tina pictured Sharon, sitting on some baby-sitting sofa, weeping on her boyfriend's shoulder. 'Poor Tina. I could have looked after her better.'

'Don't blame yourself,' said her boyfriend.

'But I do,' Sharon cried.

Tina found herself shaking her head. It wasn't Sharon's fault.

Tracey would feel bad too. Tina imagined her, lying

in bed, unable to sleep. Her mum was sitting by her, trying to soothe her.

'She was the best friend anyone could have and I was horrible to her,' sobbed Tracey. 'It was all my fault.'

'There, there,' said her mum. 'It wasn't your fault. These things happen.'

Tina was really enjoying herself. By now the tears were rolling down her face, but she was feeling warm and appreciated. For the first time she was in control, directing everyone else as if they were in her film. She fast-forwarded to the funeral.

Everyone was there, dressed in black. People from the street, teachers from school, friends and family, crowding around the open grave, crying or looking sad.

By the graveside stood her mum and dad, together again at last, with Sharon. In the background Helen and Kev stood side by side. They made an unlikely looking couple, Tina had to admit, but it kept everything tidy. Joanne and Tracey, heads together, talked quietly, reminding each other of Tina's many good points.

She dwelt for a moment on the touching scene and then moved in closer to peep into the coffin. Inside lay Tina herself, dressed in a long white nightgown, edged with lace. In her hair, which mysteriously had grown much longer and turned golden, were white flowers. She looked more like a bridesmaid than a corpse. She concentrated harder and saw herself smiling peacefully at those left behind. She wanted them to know that she forgave them.

For several minutes Tina enjoyed this sad but satisfying ending and felt very proud of the part she had played in bringing it about. Her face was wet with tears, and yet she leaned her head back against the wall and began to smile. This broad smile fixed itself on her face, as she daydreamed on.

Even a moment later, when the door of the shed suddenly and violently flew open and someone burst in, her face didn't move. She was caught out, smiling idiotically into space. Through her mind ran the common warning, 'You want to be careful or your face'll stick like that.'

nineteen

Joanne tiptoed along the school corridor, trying to prevent her footsteps echoing around the empty building. Mrs Trask had kept her waiting ages and by the time she'd finished with her everyone else had gone home. She reached the door and looked warily out. It was a slim hope, but she was praying that the two boys might have got fed up with waiting for her and gone.

They had certainly got bored, leaning against the school gates. More than once the caretaker, in passing, had asked them, 'Haven't you got homes to go to?'

Joanne's hope died when she spotted them still there. They were passing the time kicking a football around. A small first year boy was standing waiting for them to give it back. He'd been waiting ten minutes already.

'Aw, come on. I'm going to be in dead trouble with my mam if I'm late home.'

'I'd write you a note,' said Nick Insley, dribbling the ball past Barry Gibson and going on to score a goal against the wall of the caretaker's bungalow, 'but unfortunately I sprained my wrist.'

Barry Gibson fell about laughing; he was easily amused. It was one of the things Nick Insley liked about him.

There was a netball match taking place across the yard and quite a lot of people had stayed behind to watch. While both boys had their backs to her, Joanne took her chance. Under cover of the match, she edged around the school yard and along the wall, as far as the gate.

She walked quickly out of the gates and down the road, keeping close to the garden fences. She didn't really breathe freely until she was nearly at the end of the road. She thought it was probably safe at this point to break into a run. It was a mistake; they spotted her.

She heard their furious shouts. 'Hey, look. Isn't that her? The crafty little bag. Come on.'

'You just wait, Baggley.' But of course Joanne didn't.

She ran as fast as she could, which wasn't anything like fast enough. She cursed her own lack of fitness and, not for the first time, wished she could swop some of her brains for a little bit of physical skill.

She knew they would soon gain on her and she desperately tried to think what she could do. The idea of running up someone's path and throwing herself on their doorbell went through her mind, but she dismissed it as stupid. With her luck there would be nobody in.

She thought of hiding behind a hedge, hoping they'd go running by, as she'd seen people in films do. This would give her chance to double back and run into school to tell Mrs Trask, which was what her mum had suggested she should do in the first place. But Joanne reckoned that even those brainless idiots wouldn't fall for that. She needed a proper hiding place. She couldn't think where.

She risked losing a moment's advantage, turning to see how far behind they were. It was worse than she'd thought. They were less than a hundred metres away. She felt like a hunted animal about to be cornered by a pair of savage hounds. She knew that having to chase her would have made the boys angrier still. She couldn't bear to think of them getting hold of her, let alone what they might do after that. It was the stubbornness in her which kept her going. She couldn't let herself give in to them.

She was nearly through the new estate and half way home but she knew she wouldn't make it. A corner came up and she turned sharply right. Suddenly she had a plan in mind. It was only a small hope and it was all she had left. She prayed that she would remember which entry it was. If she chose the wrong one, she wouldn't get a second chance.

It took an enormous effort for Tina to rearrange her expression so that it registered the horror and surprise she felt when she saw Joanne standing in the doorway facing her.

Joanne was panting too much to speak at first. She looked awful, like a caricature of someone about to have a heart attack. She seemed as surprised to see Tina as Tina was to see her. She stumbled into the shed, closing the door behind her.

'Those hateful pigs are after me,' she finally gasped.

Tina didn't speak. She was too angry to put her words together in any sort of order. Her mind was racing through several questions. How had Joanne found her den? Had she followed her? How could she have, Tina had left ages ago? Had Nick Insley and Barry Gibson seen her? Would they crash in the next minute and wreck the place? Even if they didn't it would never be the same from now on, once they knew where it was. Joanne had managed it again. She'd dragged Tina into another mess.

'What are you doing here?' Tina demanded at last. 'How did you find me? Did you follow me?'

Joanne looked very uncomfortable. 'I didn't know you'd be here. I thought you'd have gone home.'

Tina still didn't understand, 'But what are you doing here? This is my shed.'

'There was nowhere else to go. They were right behind me...'

Exactly on cue both girls heard running footsteps coming down the street. Then they stopped. They heard the boys call out, 'Where are you, Baggy? It's no use hiding. We're going to find you. And when we do we're going to murder you.'

t w e n t y

Joanne tripped over things as she tried to find somewhere to hide. She got into a corner and slid down until she was partly hidden by a stack of wooden plant trays. She put her hands over her face, like a small child who thinks by covering her own eyes she makes herself disappear. Her breath was loud and snatched. Tina had never seen anyone this afraid before. It embarrassed her and unaccountably made her even angrier with Joanne.

'I want to know how you found me.'

'I followed you, weeks ago,' Joanne whispered. 'I wanted to find out where you went every time you disappeared...' her voice gave way and she swallowed the end of the sentence.

Tina was furious at this. She wanted to tell Joanne to clear off and not to come back but she couldn't do it. Instead she snapped at her, 'I don't know what you're so scared of; you know they're all talk.'

But when they heard the boys' footsteps coming down the entry, each of the girls fell silent and held her breath. Joanne kept on staring at Tina, silently pleading with her not to give her away. She started to cry; Tina looked down.

'She's got to be hiding somewhere,' said Nick Insley. 'She couldn't have got far ahead of us. She'd have to have moved faster than greased lightning.' The two boys started sniggering.

'She couldn't run to save her life,' said Barry Gibson. 'She's like one of them spastics.' And he did an imitation of a handicapped person trying to run. Then they both limped around grunting, in a horrible parody of physical disability.

'Spaggy Baggley, where are you?' called Nick Insley.

At that moment Tina hated them. She was glad she couldn't see them; hearing them was bad enough. She felt the anger suddenly flare up, as if someone had lit a fuse inside her. She wasn't going to let anyone push her around any more; she'd already had too much of feeling powerless.

The boys were right outside by now and one of them had his hand on the door. She heard Barry Gibson's voice. 'I bet she's in here.'

Tina couldn't let the boys see Joanne, not in this state. She could hardly bear to look at her herself. She thrust Sammy into Joanne's hands and rushed to the door. She pulled it open and stepped outside before the boys could come in. She walked straight into Barry Gibson, who nearly fell over in surprise.

'What do you want?' she snarled at him and gave him a push. He stumbled backwards. 'Well?' She pushed him again. He was too stunned to answer.

But Nick Insley recovered quite quickly from his surprise. 'We want that bag of a sister of yours.'

Tina let the 'sister' pass. She wasn't going to waste her breath on *him*. 'She's not here.'

'I bet she is.'

'She's not.'

'Well, we'll soon see,' he said, coming forward.

'Like hell you will! You can clear off and take him with you.' She pushed Barry Gibson once more in the ribs and he began to laugh, partly from embarrassment, partly because he was actually very ticklish and unused to girls touching him.

'Hey, pack it in,' he laughed. Then he backed off and went to lean against the wall of the house.

Tina stood there, staring them out, daring them to make another move forward. Nick Insley stared back at her and when he saw Tina's little hands made into angry fists he nearly laughed out loud. 'Who do you think you're kidding?'

Tina was getting more and more worked up. 'You think you can push anyone around, don't you, you greasy overgrown slug. Well, you lay a hand on me and I swear my dad'll break your neck.'

Tina had no idea if this was true, but she didn't

care. She had enough stored up anger to do the job herself, and she was working up to it nicely.

For a moment Nick Insley seemed uncertain how to react. She was only a girl, and not very big at that, but he'd never seen this side of her before. There was more stifled laughter behind him. He glanced back and the two boys grinned at each other. They didn't move.

'Well, what are you waiting for? Clear off,' Tina shouted.

Her face was crimson and the yelling had made all the veins in her neck stand out. She was almost spitting the words at them. She looked a bit like someone ready to have a fit.

Nick Insley changed his approach. 'Look, this is nothing to do with you. It's that bitch of a sister of yours we want. I thought you hated her an' all.'

'There's only one person around here I hate and that's you, you pathetic excuse for a human being. You and that soft ape go about pretending to be tough, when you're nothing but a pair of cowards, picking on girls. Well, I'm not scared of you, either of you. You'll go in this shed over my dead body.'

The words Tina used were as much a surprise to her as they were to the boys. They didn't seem to belong to her, but even so they felt right, they were telling the boys exactly what she wanted to say.

Despite her size she didn't appear such a joke now and Nick Insley turned to see what Barry Gibson was up to; he was worried that he might have disappeared.

'It's no use looking at him. He won't help you.'

Nick stared directly at Barry Gibson, who just shrugged his shoulders and wore his habitual silly grin.

'What d'you mean?'

'Ask him.'

Barry Gibson had turned almost as red as Tina. He knew what she was up to; she was going to tell Nick Insley about the Valentine card, and the letter he'd hidden today in her coat pocket. He would never live it down. He pretended to be mystified by all this, but he looked away rather than catch Nick's eye.

'What's going on?'

'Nothing,' said Barry Gibson. 'Come on, let's go home; I've had enough of this. I've got better things to do than hang around here with you.'

'What are you talking about?' Nick Insley said, grabbing hold of him by the jacket. 'Have you forgotten what we came for?'

'Get off me.' Barry pushed Nick Insley against the wall of the shed, rather harder than he'd intended.

There was a crashing sound as a stack of wooden seed trays inside fell to the floor, but neither of the boys paid it any attention. They held onto each other's clothes and tried to push each other over.

'You're soft on her! That's it, isn't it?' Nick Insley scoffed. 'You'd make a good pair, two thickos together.'

'Well, she's right about you, it's a wimp's trick hitting girls.'

'Who the hell are you calling a wimp, you moron?'

The boys were now rolling on the ground, locked so tightly in a bear hug they couldn't swing a fist back to actually hit each other. They were puffing and grunting and getting angrier by the minute.

'Stop it, both of you,' screamed Tina. 'Clear off and fight somewhere else.'

But the boys ignored her and kept on struggling. It was hopeless. Even though this new development meant that her own problems were temporarily solved, she couldn't stand by and watch the boys fighting.

Suddenly Nick Insley levered himself up and got on top of Barry Gibson, pinning him down with his own weight. He took hold of his head and started banging it on the ground. He looked as if he might never stop. Tina rushed forward and tried to pull him off.

'Pack it in, you'll hurt him.'

He let go just long enough to push her over, but she kept coming back. Although she managed to stop him for a minute or two, she couldn't really move him, no matter how much she tugged. She tried to sink her teeth into him but she only ended up with a mouthful of denim jacket.

'Get off,' he snarled and sent her flying again.

Behind the shed door Joanne was still shaking. She could hear a struggle going on outside, but she couldn't work out exactly what was happening. It sounded as though Barry Gibson and Nick Insley were scrapping and Tina was trying to stop them. Joanne couldn't imagine why. If she'd been Tina she'd have let them get on with it. She'd have taken the chance to make a getaway. Joanne would have sneaked out now and raced off home herself, if she'd thought she could get past them unnoticed a second time.

She had been amazed to hear some of the things Tina had said to the boys. She hadn't realised Tina had it in her. Joanne had always thought of herself as so much stronger than Tina, and braver than most, but she wasn't sure about that any more. Although she could hardly bear to admit it, she knew she couldn't have stood up to them like Tina had.

The door burst open; Joanne shot across the shed and cowered in the corner. Tina stared at her and barely hid her contempt. 'Come on, you've got to help me. I think he's going to kill him.'

Joanne shook her head. 'Let him; I don't care.'

'Don't be so stupid.'

'They'll start on me then.'

'Just stop thinking about yourself for once. Now come on. This is serious. Anyway, you owe me a favour.'

She grabbed Joanne by the jacket and dragged her outside. The two girls took an arm each and heaved. This time Nick Insley had no free arm to hit them with and he lost his balance. He fell backwards. He rolled over and was up in a second, but so was Barry Gibson. The girls threw themselves onto Nick Insley before he had the chance to attack.

'Stop it,' Tina yelled. 'Stop being stupid. You call yourselves mates and yet now you're trying to murder each other!'

Nick Insley would have carried on; Barry Gibson had more sense. He dragged his jacket back on.

'I'm going,' he said.

He slunk off down the entry before Nick Insley could start again, swinging his arms in a carefree manner. As he reached the street, in an effort to cover up his damaged pride, he turned and grinned at them all, then he kept on walking.

The girls had managed to split them up long enough for Barry Gibson to see sense, but Nick Insley was still in such a temper he didn't know what to do with himself. He pushed each of the girls away, sending them flying. Next he kicked the shed hard; a jagged hole appeared in the rotten wood. Soon he was kicking everything in sight. He swung out at some old dustbins. One fell over with a terrible clatter; the other, which was actually full of builders' rubble, never even moved. It seemed likely, by the expression on his face, that he might have broken his toe.

He hugged his injured foot and danced around on the other one while he cursed in a long, satisfying stream of bad language. As soon as he could bear to put his foot down and walk on it, he hobbled off up the entry.

The girls took one look at each other and started to laugh. Soon they couldn't stop. They leaned against a wall for support; the sense of relief made them dizzy.

They couldn't believe the danger was over. Nick Insley had hardly noticed Joanne. She could see now that he was so full of anger that he was always looking for someone to take it out on; anyone who crossed his path would do. He might well pick on her again tomorrow or next week, but having seen him hugging his big toe and howling obscenities she would never be able to take him completely seriously.

Once the joke was exhausted the girls became quiet and awkward with one another. Tina suddenly remembered the hamster.

'Where's Sammy? What did you do with him?'

'I put him back in his cage. What's he doing here anyway?'

Tina sighed. Was there no getting away from Joanne? Here she was again interfering in her affairs, spoiling her plans. But she was most furious with her now because Joanne was reminding Tina of things she'd been happy to forget for a while; they all came flooding back.

Tina didn't answer her, but Joanne persisted. 'And what have you got in that bag? It looked like clothes. Are you thinking of going somewhere?'

twenty-one

Tina gave Joanne a warning look. She wanted her to know that she was going too far.

'I wasn't looking,' Joanne assured her. 'The bag was open and it was right by me. I couldn't help seeing, honest.'

Tina wasn't interested in Joanne's excuses and she decided to ignore her questions. Tina wanted some explanations herself.

'I want to know why you followed me.'

'I just wanted to know where you went, that's all. It's not a crime, is it?'

'It's none of your business,' Tina snapped back. 'If you must know, I came here to get away from you.'

'It's not my fault we have to share a room. I don't like it either, you know.'

'You don't hate it as much as I do.'

'Well I do, actually.'

Here they were again – stalemate.

Tina turned her back on Joanne and went inside the shed. Joanne followed her. Tina let out a little gasp when she realised that the fallen wooden trays were now burying Sammy's cage. She pulled them away frantically and uncovered him. At first she couldn't see the hamster, cocooned in layers of shredded paper. Once more he'd slept through all the excitement.

'Is he OK?'

'Yes,' Tina snapped. She didn't add 'no thanks to you' but it hung in the air. The girls stood there awkwardly, not speaking.

'I suppose I should say thanks for covering up for me just now,' said Joanne at last.

'It was more than you did for me at school.'

This was true and Joanne had no excuse, so she said nothing. Tina suspected that this silence was the nearest to an apology she was likely to get; Joanne wasn't very good at admitting fault.

There was another difficult pause while Tina waited for Joanne to go, now that she had no excuse to stay. She looked at her watch as a hint, but Joanne didn't take it.

Instead she tried again. 'It's really good, this shed.'

'Mmm,' said Tina.

'What do you do here?'

'Nothing much.'

'You must do something.'

'I mind my own business, mostly.'

But Joanne wouldn't be put off. 'Does anyone else know about it?'

'Only the two worst people on earth – thanks to you!'

Joanne went quiet until her curiosity again got the better of her.

'I still don't understand what you want your clothes for.'

'I was running away!' Tina yelled at her. 'Now are you happy?'

'But what for?' Joanne asked, genuinely surprised. 'I thought you said you were going back to your mum soon.'

'Well, now I'm not. Any more questions?'

Tina watched Joanne's face carefully for the first sign of a smirk but Joanne's response surprised her. 'I've thought about it as well. Lots of times.'

'You?'

'Yeah, why not. I hate living in our house as well, you know. After this trouble at school I would have gone too, if there'd been anywhere to go.'

Tina sat down and took this in. Where did people run away to, when they were only thirteen-year-old kids like them? If someone as clever as Joanne couldn't work it out, there couldn't be an easy answer. She sighed.

'So are you really going?' Joanne asked.

'Why do you want to know?' Tina asked.

'You'd better give me the key, that's all. I'm already going to be in trouble, when my mum gets in and there's no tea.'

Now it was Tina's turn to look uncomfortable.

'I haven't got it.'

'Well, where is it?'

'I put it through the door.'

'So how do I get in?' Joanne's voice rose for the first time.

'I don't know and I don't care.'

'I'm telling you my mum'll hit the roof. Look, it's gone five!'

'You'd better go then, hadn't you?'

But even now Joanne seemed unprepared to leave. She leaned against the door as if she was waiting for something. Tina could see she wasn't going to get rid of her.

'Where are you thinking of going?' Joanne asked.

'Oh, just shut up, will you,' Tina said. She had no answers to any of Joanne's questions and she was almost at the end of her patience.

What was the point of carrying this on? She *had* nowhere else to go. And anyway she was for too tired to run away. Tina felt as though she'd been living under siege for weeks, but she could see the worst was over. This must be what it felt like if you survived a war. At least you discovered you were still alive.

Joanne watched Tina, trying to guess what she was thinking.

'If we're quick and we go now, we might get in

before her,' she suggested. 'We could tell her we had a detention.'

This reminded Tina that she actually had, but hadn't gone. She looked at Joanne to see what had happened.

'Oh... Mrs Trask said she would look forward to the pleasure of hearing *your* version of events tomorrow. Don't worry, though, I'll tell her what happened.'

'You'd better,' said Tina

'I will, honest. So are you coming home then?'

'Do I have any choice?'

Both girls knew the answer to that. They picked up their bags and let themselves out.

As she closed the door of the shed, Tina wondered whether she would ever bother coming back here, now that everybody and his auntie knew about it. She struggled with her bags and the hamster cage, rearranging them into the best position.

'I'll carry that,' Joanne offered.

'I can manage,' said Tina.

When they emerged from the entry the girls spotted Barry Gibson leaning against a lamp-post across the road. Joanne immediately began to panic.

'Take no notice,' Tina said under her breath. 'Pretend you haven't seen him.'

It was difficult to make this entirely convincing, but

the girls looked straight ahead and walked on. As they turned the corner Joanne couldn't resist a glance back.

'He's still following us.'

'So what. You're surely not scared of him.'

'Not him on his own...'

'Well then.'

'Does he really fancy you?'

Tina pretended she hadn't heard.

'Are you going to go out with him?'

Tina silenced Joanne with a warning look, and walked on.

Barry Gibson had almost given up and gone home. He was cold and his stomach had been telling him that it was nearly teatime. It was a far more accurate measurer of time than his watch, which was pinched and had never been very reliable. It had taught him one important lesson: never to nick off the market; they were a load of rogues that ran those stalls. Still, he liked to wear it, even if it didn't work; he felt it improved his image.

He was relieved when the girls finally emerged. He was afraid they were going to stay in there for hours. He had been hoping that Tina might come out on her own. He had been working up his courage to speak to her. But now she had that scarecrow with her he knew he didn't dare. He thought it wouldn't hurt to follow her, though. She might not have found his note yet.

Every time he remembered what she'd called Nick Insley he laughed out loud: a greasy overgrown slug, that was really wicked, because it was spot on. He wished he could think of things like that. He'd always fancied Tina; after this afternoon he was mad about her. He couldn't wait for a chance to put his arm round her. Just thinking about her was making his chest ache.

He was scared, not knowing whether she'd tell him to get lost and then laugh at him to her friends. But he had a feeling she wasn't that kind of girl. He kept on following her.

'Do you want half of this?' asked Joanne.

She offered a broken chocolate bar to Tina. It reminded her how hungry she was. She didn't want to take it, she was still angry with Joanne, but it looked too tempting to refuse.

'Where did you get it?'

'I bought it, of course, with my pocket money.'

'I thought you saved all your money in the bank.'

'Some of it, I do. It depends on how bad the food's been.'

Tina couldn't believe her ears. She imagined what Helen would say if she heard this revelation. 'Don't you like it either?'

'Lentil rissoles, are you dreaming?' said Joanne.

'But you eat them. You eat everything.'

'That doesn't mean I enjoy it.'

'Why don't you tell her, she's your mum?'

'Don't you think I've tried? It's not worth it. She's got this thing about kids being faddy. It's because she was. As a kid she'd hardly eat anything.'

'You'd think she'd understand then.'

'I know, but she was a horror. She used to spit things out. Then her mum died when she was only six and she's felt guilty about it ever since. She hates it if I leave anything.'

'That's awful.'

'Oh, it's been much easier lately.'

'I hadn't noticed.'

'Well, you're so much pickier it makes me look good. I just have to keep my head down and you get told off.'

'You're a born creep,' said Tina

'Huh, that's good coming from you. Don't think I haven't noticed you sneaking into the kitchen sometimes to get in with my mum.'

Tina blushed. She had tried at times to be helpful to Helen, but it hadn't seemed to get her anywhere.

They were nearly home now. Tina had been so slowed down by the hamster cage she'd had to let Joanne take one of her bags. They still had their shadow, but neither of the girls acknowledged him.

'Why aren't you going home to your mum?' Joanne finally got around to asking.

Tina didn't want to tell her, but soon she would find out anyway. 'She's having a baby.'

'Are you kidding?'

Tina couldn't be bothered going into it all. 'So that'll be enough for Kev, without me living there as well. He's not keen on kids. At least the baby'll be his.'

Tina waited for one of Joanne's cutting comments but Joanne said nothing. They walked on in silence.

'Anyhow,' she added. 'I was never mad on the idea of living with Kev.'

Tina surprised herself. This was the first time she'd faced the fact of never going home again, without wanting to sob. And she knew now that this meant she would have to stay at Helen's. She considered it, as if it was something she could actually bear to do, and realised it was.

The worst part of living at Helen's had been Joanne. Tina had learnt a lot about Joanne lately. She knew that Joanne was cleverer than her in some ways, but definitely not in others. She wasn't any braver or stronger, in fact underneath she'd been just as scared and confused. Until today Tina had been afraid of Joanne; not any more.

'I think it's time we had a few rules about our

room,' she said.

'What do you mean "our" room?'

'Our bedroom,' said Tina. 'Do you know one of the things I hate most about sharing with you is the way you always turn the lamp on and off, whenever *you* feel like it, as if you're the Keeper of the Light.'

'All you ever do is lie there, sucking your thumb. What difference does it make?'

'I'm thinking, if you must know, and I think better with the light off.'

'What're you thinking about?'

Tina tapped the end of her nose with her finger. 'I have to share a room with you; I don't have to let you climb inside my head and inspect my brain as well.'

This silenced Joanne, but only for a while. She had a couple of complaints herself. 'The thing I hate most is that hamster. Well, not the hamster, I've got used to him; it's the smell. You ought to clean him out more; it's disgusting.'

Tina opened her mouth to protest; one look from Joanne told her not to bother. They knew that hygiene was not Tina's strong point.

'And another thing...' said Joanne.

'Just a minutes,' said Tina, 'my turn next...'

By the time the girls reached home they were still bickering. But when they tried the door they fell silent. It was already unlocked. They walked in, leaving their things in the hall. They could see through to the kitchen. The morning's mess was exactly as they'd left it. Helen was standing with her back to them leaning against the sink.

There was something in the set of her shoulders that told them how depressed she felt. They hovered in the doorway, uncertain whether to go in. At last she heard them and turned round. When she spoke there was a tightness about her voice which made the girls swallow, as if to clear their own throats.

'And where on earth do you think you two have been?'

twenty-two

Neither of the girls answered. They both felt ashamed. Their detention excuse seemed inadequate now.

'After all I said this morning...' Her voice rose quickly to a shout. 'Look at this mess. How could you!'

They stood rigid with fear in the doorway. They had expected trouble, but nothing like this. Helen looked fit to murder them. Just over a few dirty pots and the tea not ready? Tina couldn't believe it.

'Where have you been for an hour and a half?... Answer me!'

She clenched her fists as if this was the only way she could keep herself from striking them. They didn't know what to say. The room was very quiet after the shouting and for a few seconds they could hear Helen's breathing. Joanne had never seen her mum so angry; it scared her.

'Mum, I'm sorry,' she said.

It was what Helen needed to hear. She put her hand to her face. 'Grandad died this afternoon,' she said. It was all the explanation she could manage.

Joanne went on standing there. A moment ago

she'd been fixed to the spot with fear; now even though the fear had passed she couldn't have moved if she'd wanted to.

Helen stood at the sink, trying to hold back the tears. In her hand was a screwed up tea-towel. She held it to her face to hide her pain.

Tina glanced at Joanne to see what she would do, but Joanne was still stunned. No one spoke; no one moved.

Tina took in the picture of the three of them, caught there in the kitchen, like a group of statues. Although it lasted just for a matter of moments she saw quite clearly that this was how they'd lived for most of a year, each of them in their own way unable to make a move towards the others, as if their feelings were frozen.

It took quite an effort for Tina to take the first step, but she knew she was the only one who could do it. She went over to Helen and put her arms round her. She was so straight and unbending that it felt as awkward as hugging a piece of furniture. But Tina kept her arms round her and looked up into Helen's sad face. Her own face was already wet with tears.

'I'm really sorry, Helen,' she said. 'You must feel very sad.'

And the words seemed to release Helen. She let go of the tea-towel and leaned heavily against Tina, who had to brace herself to take the unexpected weight. She sobbed, her shoulders rising and falling with the effort. And the tears broke loose at last.

Tina patted Helen's shoulder; otherwise she just stood there supporting her. She turned her head, so that she could see Joanne. What was she still waiting for, Tina wondered? Even now she seemed to be unable to move.

Tina gently shook her head back to get Joanne to come over too. But Joanne frowned to show she didn't understand.

Mega-brain strikes again, thought Tina. How could anyone be so slow?

She made the same beckoning movement and this time Joanne understood. She came forward and put her arms round her mum and Tina made room for her. For a while the three of them stood locked together in an awkward group. Since neither of the girls could think of the right things to say, they stayed silent, holding Helen while she cried.

After a few minutes Tina tried to indicate to Joanne, through a sideways head movement, that she should take her mum into the living room, to sit down in a comfortable chair. Again Joanne looked at Tina as if she was trying to communicate in Chinese. 'Why don't you go and sit next door,' said Tina, making encouraging faces at Joanne, 'and I'll make us all a cup of tea.'

'No, I can't,' said Helen. 'There's no meal on yet and Dave'll be in any minute.'

'Yes, you can,' said Joanne, steering her through the door. 'He can wait. Come on.'

She led her mum into the living room and Tina stayed in the kitchen. She put on the kettle, laid out the mugs and then set about finishing the washing up. Well, she thought, this feels like old times: coming home to find her own mum in a state, having to sort things out before her dad got in.

She quickly tidied up the breakfast mess and cleared the kitchen. She knew she could have done more to help Helen these last few months. Even though Helen sometimes behaved as if she was Superwoman, Tina could see now that she wasn't. Nobody should have to be more than just human. Funny, she thought, how they had all been so busy pretending to be what they were not, Helen, Joanne...

What had she pretended to be, she wondered? The quiet little mouse, trying to please everyone and keep out of trouble? Or the little martyr, like Tracey had said, behaving as if the whole world was against her, as if she was the only one who had anything to be unhappy about.

Tina hadn't had time to notice she was still wearing her coat. As she took it off, out of habit she checked her pockets. She found a letter with her name on it in a very childish hand. She recognised it and immediately blushed. Turning to check there was no one there she opened it and read:

I think your wunderful will you go out with me
I'll be outside your howse at seven tonihgt

Tina almost laughed aloud. The minute she'd read it she wanted to get rid of the note, so that she could pretend it had never been sent. She was tempted to tear it up and eat it, like she'd seen spies do, in comics. But before she could, the back door opened and her dad came in from work. He put his lunch box on the worktop and left his coat on the door handle. Tina stuffed the note back in her pocket. She turned to pour the tea. Dave came over and kissed her.

'Where's Helen?'

'She's in there. I've just made her some tea. She's a bit upset; her dad died today.'

'Oh heck,' said Dave. He moved as if to go through to her, but Tina stopped him.

'She's all right. She just needed a good cry.'

'OK,' said Dave. He looked into Tina's face. He could see she was trying to tell him something else.

'Joanne's with her; she's fine... Why don't we leave them on their own for a bit, eh?'

Dave nodded as he began to understand what Tina was saying.

'Good idea.'

'You dry up,' said Tina, 'and I'll take the tea through, then you and me can go and get some fish and chips.'

'Fish and chips?'

'It'll be nice and easy and it'll give Helen a break. She's been working too hard lately.'

Dave smiled, picked up the tea-towel, saluted and clicked his heels to attention. 'Whatever you say, Boss Cat.'

'And you can hang that coat up properly as well,' she said.

In the living room Helen and Joanne sat side by side on the sofa.

'Here you are,' said Tina. 'This'll make you feel better. Me and my dad are taking care of the tea.'

'Thanks,' said Helen.

'Did you put sugar in mine? I can't drink it without,' said Joanne.

'I know that,' said Tina. 'I've been living here nine months, I ought to.'

Helen smiled and they each took a mug from her. Then she left them alone again. After all the crying Helen felt sleepy and relaxed. Joanne was leaning against her mum.

'I'm sorry about this morning, love,' said Helen. 'How did you get on with those boys? Was it OK?'

'Oh, that, yeah,' said Joanne, dismissively. It felt as

if it had happened weeks ago. 'Boys like that, they're all talk.'

When Tina came back into the kitchen, Dave said, 'Did you know one of those lads is outside?'

'Is he still there?'

'Who is he?'

'Oh, nobody. He's in our class at school.'

'What happened to the other one?'

'We got rid of him. At least this one's harmless.'

'What's he doing out there?'

'He's waiting for seven o'clock.'

'He's got a long wait. Can't he tell the time?'

'Probably not, he's pretty thick.'

'Shall I see if he wants to come in for a cuppa?' Dave suggested.

'No!' said Tina. 'Don't give him any encouragement, he's stupid enough already.'

'You can't leave the poor lad out there; it's raining.'

'Oh yes I can,' said Tina. 'Just ignore him and he'll go away.'

'You are a hard woman,' said Dave.

'Yes, I know,' she said, grinning. 'I am, aren't I.'

more black apples to

get your teeth into...

Jerry Spinelli
1 84121 926 6
£4.99

Stargirl. She's as magical as the desert sky. As mysterious as her own name.

Nobody knows who she is,
or where she's come from.
But everyone loves her for being
different. And she captures
Leo's heart with just one smile.

But standing out from the crowd isn't always admired. And when people start to turn against them, Stargirl and Leo are forced to test the strength of their love.

Celebrating non-conformity and the thrill of first love, Stargirl is a classic of our time.

"This is going to be huge and it deserves to be"
THE GUARDIAN

"The striking and charismatic central character is wonderfully
non-conformist, unique and not easily summarised.
This is an unforgettable book"
THE BOOKSELLER

*"The magical quality of this unusual and original story
has taken the American market by storm, and looks
set to do the same here. Like its whimsical heroine,
this is a story which, once read, is not easily forgotten"*
TIME OUT

"Could match the success of Artemis Fowl"
THE BOOKSELLER

"A novel as brilliant and bracing as a fireworks display; a joyful,
tender, fizzy celebration of diversity and non-conformity, with a
heroine whose euphoric dynamism effects everyone she comes into
contact with - especially the reader"
CAROUSEL

WHSmith Children's Book of the Year Shortlisted

*"This truly remarkable book is set to take schools, bookshops and
libraries by storm. Spinelli is an accomplished writer whose magical prose
enchants the reader... This may be a book written for children but it is
one that adults will enjoy with equal vigour"*
WATERSTONE'S

"This book champions individuality, but shows us the price
of non-conformity. A must read for today's children"
CHILDREN'S BOOKSHOP, HUDDERSFIELD

*"What a treat! Stargirl is a real gem...
Her story has more than a touch of magic"*
WENDY COOLING

"An original high-school drama that blasts
through teenage love of conformity"
The Sunday Times

Andrew Matthews
1 84121 758 1
£4.99

'Anna? I'd like you to meet Pete...'

Pete may be gorgeous, but he's very unfriendly.
Anyway, Anna's got other things on her mind.
Sent away for the summer to stop her seeing her
boyfriend, Anna is pining for her lost love.

At first.

But then she gets involved in the local wolf
sanctuary, and discovers a thrilling and dangerous
passion. A passion that eventually throws her
and Pete together in a time of crisis.

'Young love, teen angst, funky grannies and wolves.
What more d'ya need?'
Mizz

Andrew Matthews
1 84121 077 4
£4.99

At first Danni doesn't think anything of it.
After all, people get wrong numbers all the time...

But as the mysterious phone calls continue, she
starts to get the feeling she is being watched.

When her old friend, Leah, turns up out of the
blue, Danni is glad of the distraction. But Leah's
strange behaviour drags up disturbing memories
that Danni has long hidden from herself.

She is haunted by the half-remembered...until
finally she is forced to confront the nightmare.

orchard black apples

jerry spinelli:

Crash	1 84121 222 9
Stargirl	1 84121 926 6

brian keaney:

Balloon House	1 84121 437 X
Bitter Fruit	1 84121 005 6
Family Secrets	1 84121 530 9
Falling for Joshua	1 84121 858 8
The Private Life of Georgia Brown	1 84121 528 7

andrew matthews:

Shadow of the Wolf	1 84121 077 4
Wolf Summer	1 84121 758 1

jean ure:

Get a Life!	1 84121 831 6

linda newbery:

No Way Back	1 84121 582 1
Breaktime	1 84121 584 8
Windfall	1 84121 586 4

All priced at £4.99
Orchard Black Apples are available from all good bookshops,
or can be ordered direct from the publisher:
Orchard Books, PO BOX 29, Douglas IM99 1BQ
Credit card orders please telephone 01624 836000
or fax 01624 837033 or visit our Internet site: www.wattspub.co.uk
or e-mail: bookshop@enterprise.net for details.

To order please quote title, author and ISBN
and your full name and address.
Cheques and postal orders should be made payable to 'Bookpost plc.'
Postage and packing is FREE within the UK
(overseas customers should add £1.00 per book).

Prices and availability are subject to change.